The Best of Eddie Kantar

Granovetter Books
18 Village View Bluff
Ballston Lake, NY 12019
(518) 899-6670

Printed in the United States of America
ISBN 0-940257-03-3

Contents

Photos

Aᴠᴀɪʟᴀʙʟᴇ Bᴏᴏᴋs ʙʏ Eᴅᴅɪᴇ Kᴀɴᴛᴀʀ

Bridge Bidding Made Easy
Bridge Conventions
Defensive Bridge Play Complete
An Expert's Guide to Improving Your Bidding Skills
Introduction to Declarer's Play
Introduction to Defender's Play
Kantar for the Defense Volume 1
Kantar for the Defense Volume 2
Gamesman Bridge (with Jackson Stanley)
A New Approach to Play and Defense Volume 1
A New Approach to Play and Defense Volume 2
Test Your Play Volume 1
Test Your Play Volume 2
20 Kantar Lessons

Foreword

ANYONE WHO READS this book is in for a treat. I had seen many of the hands previously; in fact I was involved in several myself. But I still couldn't put the book down until I had finished it.

Eddie has an unusual sense of humor. He recognizes funny *situations*—like when our opponents crossed a convention off their card after seeing how Eddie and I had mishandled it. Or the "gambit" described in this book when the opponents made the mistake of listening to our discussion after arriving in a 4-1 trump fit. They "profited" by our experience in running from a doubled contract with a 5-5 trump fit into a doubled contract with a 4-2 trump fit. Since they were doubled and we were not, our "gambit" (unintentional, of course) paid off.

Eddie taught me a new suit combination. Suppose the contract is four spades and the hearts are distributed as follows:

$$\begin{array}{c} \text{Dummy} \\ \heartsuit\ 10\ 7\ 4 \end{array}$$

West   East
$\heartsuit$ 9 8 2 $\heartsuit$ K J 6 5 3

$$\begin{array}{c} \text{Declarer} \\ \heartsuit\ A\ Q \end{array}$$

West leads the nine of hearts on opening lead, ducked around to declarer's queen. The next time West is on lead, he leads the heart eight, dummy plays the ten, East the jack, and declarer ruffs! About ten seconds later declarer (Eddie, of course) says, "Oh, I've got a heart," and he plays the ace. In the meantime East and West glare at each other, both thinking they are playing with the most hopeless idiot ever inflicted upon a bridge player.

In this book you will see top experts making bids and plays they had hoped would never come to light. Eddie pokes fun at the greatest, Bob Hamman in particular. None of this anonymous stuff. No matter how bad the play, all names are given. But how can anyone complain when Eddie is harder on himself than on anyone else?

I guarantee that you will enjoy this book!

—MARSHALL MILES
1989

Author's Preface

I HAVE ENOUGH TROUBLE writing forewords to other people's books, let alone my own.

However, to give you some idea of what awaits you within, I have tried to collect all the published articles I have written that my friends have told me are funny.

Additionally, I have taken several liberties. First, I have decided to rerun two of the stories that appeared in Bridge Humor. The first, "My Father's Son," deals with my experiences in teaching. The second, "Ceci and Me," still has people coming up to me and asking, "Is there really a Ceci?" Yes, there is.

All but two of the other stories have appeared in The Bulletin, Popular Bridge, Bridge Today, The Bridge Set and The Bridge World. "Reprieve" and "The Flight Home" are in print here for the first time.

I have also included two articles, one written by Matthew Granovetter and the other by Fred Turner, that left me weak from laughter when I read them. I hope they have the same effect on you.

In fact, I hope the entire book does.

—EDDIE KANTAR
LOS ANGELES, 1989

The Best of
Eddie Kantar

What's My Line?

DOES ANYONE remember the T.V. show "What's My Line?" hosted by John Daly? They dug up people with oddball occupations, and then the panel, which consisted of Bennett Cerf, Dorothy Kilgallen, Arlene Francis plus a rotating fourth, given a limited amount of time and questions, had to work out what these contestants did for a living. Somehow they usually got it right.

Nevertheless, I always thought that if I could just get on that show I could give them a run for their money. After all, how many bridge professionals were floating around at that time? Even today there are not that many.

A bridge professional is someone who derives a living entirely from the game of contract bridge. There are a number of ways to do this:

1. Teach or give seminars.
2. Play bridge for money—either at home or at bridge clubs where money bridge is played.
3. Write magazine articles, bridge columns, and books.
4. Be a hired gun.

I do all four.

The Bridge Professional as a teacher
This happens to be the way I got started. In fact, I taught my first class when I was 16 years old (is there an aura of a misspent youth here?) and I am still teaching 39 years later!

I was born in Minneapolis, 1932, to Alice and Sigmund Kantar of Paris and Romania. I learned to play bridge at the age of eleven. In high school, I started teaching my classmates. My first victims were girls who had bridge-playing boyfriends. Once they learned, I never saw them again.

My first real class (I got paid) was at the age of seventeen at the Emanuel Cohen Center in Minneapolis. Attending the University of Minnesota, I was able to work my way through college by teaching bridge at various homes.

I graduated with a major in foreign languages and today I can speak at least three or four words in Spanish, French, Italian and German. I give seminars throughout the country and presently teach two or three classes a week with an average of eighty students in each class. Out of those eighty per class, I've had some real lulus.

For example, I had one student who could only play by reciting rhymes when it was time to play a card. Here are a few of her standbys:

When the dummy is to your right, lead the
weakest suit in sight.
When the dummy is to your left, lead through heft.
Leading top of three small is worst of all.
Don't be cute, lead partner's suit.
You will lose face if you underlead an ace.
Underleading a king is a very dangerous thing.

If there wasn't a rhyme to say, this student didn't know what to play.

Then I had another lady who asked me what I thought of the Island Two-Club convention. I told her I had never heard of it. She said that it was an opening bid of two clubs that showed 18-20 high card points and was forcing for one round. Furthermore, she assured me that everybody was playing it.

I said that I thought it was some sort of regional perversion. "Well, tell me what you think of it anyway," she said, "I play with a bunch of perverts."

Then I had a "beginning" class that I had taught for only five years. I thought that perhaps they were ready to progress to the intermediate level. Just to make sure I gave them a little test. I laid out the following spade suit; hearts were trump.

```
                    North (dummy)
                    ♠ Q 7 2
West                                    East
♠ A K 6 5 4                             ♠ 9 3
                    South
                    ♠ J 10 8
```

It was a lesson on signalling vs. trump contracts and West leads the king of spades. I wanted to see how many of them would remember to start a high-low with the East hand to show a doubleton.

One lady sitting East wondered how her partner would know that the nine was her highest card. After all, couldn't she have a ten or an eleven? I put the intermediate lessons on hold after that one.

I also enjoy hearing stories form other bridge teachers. The late John Gerber used to tell this one: after teaching a series of ten lessons he sat down at his "star" table to play a few random hands.

On the very first hand John opened one notrump. His left hand opponent passed and his partner responded "two no spades." This is still the best way of showing a void suit that I have ever encountered.

In a similar vein, though I am getting ahead of myself, one of my friends was playing professionally with a particularly weak player, Alice.

My friend opened three spades and Alice had quite a good hand with seven diamonds and six clubs. Never having had a distribution like that, and sure she would never be able to tell her partner what she had, she simply put one suit in one hand and the other in the other hand and started to bid. Alice had devised the best method ever known for showing a two-suiter.

Back to the classroom. New York expert Peter Leventritt tells this one. Once while teaching a class at the famous Card School in New York, he had a fellow signed up who clearly wasn't interested in learning how to play bridge. He was there for his girlfriend's sake, period.

In fact, when the class started playing hands he never played. He just sat around, bored. Comes the seventh lesson and a few people don't show up and this fellow is forced to sit in.

On the very first hand he is the dealer with 14 high card

points plus a five card spade suit. He has an easy one spade opening bid. Silence. Eventually Peter walks over to the table and asks him what he is going to open. No answer. Peter finally discovers that this fellow doesn't even know how to count up his points. He goes over the point count and asks the fellow once more what he is going to open. No answer.

Finally, Peter says, "Go ahead, don't worry, just open anything."

"O.K., O.K., I'll open for a dollar."

The Bridge Professional as a Gambler

Of all of the ways to make a living at bridge, this is the toughest of all.

In order to be a winning player you must be the best player in the game. That means constantly being partnered by weaker players. Inevitably they are going to do things during the course of a session that will cost you money. Even though you know this is going to happen you have to control yourself or even worse things will happen to you.

Added to that are the card fees. After all, the club has to make some revenue. Those card fees can eventually eat you up. Most bridge hustlers play two sessions a day. Assuming a $10.00 card fee per session, a person can pay some $5,000 a year in card fees alone—and this does not include overtime fees. For example, you might decide to continue playing rather than eat dinner, or play on into the wee hours of the morning after the club is theoretically closed. All of this costs.

Then, of course, there are losing streaks. The typical rubber bridge player spends all the money he wins thinking he will never lose. Then it happens. Nothing goes right. You get no cards. Even when you get a good hand your partner has nothing. Suddenly your opponents produce brilliancies against you that even they didn't think they were capable of.

If you don't have the mental fortitude to handle all of this, try working. It's much easier on the nerves.

I gave about 12 years of myself to this way of life. Between the ages of 18 and 30 I could usually be found in one of two places— the Plaza Hotel in Minneapolis or the Los Angeles Bridge Club.

I got started in my home town of Minneapolis. I haunted the bridge club, playing for more than I could afford. I remember playing in a rubber bridge game where I started to give my partner, Irv Levin, some heat for something or other. "Kantar," he said, "shut up. You are the only person in this club who is overboard at a tenth, and I don't want to hear from you." I shut up.

Then I moved to Los Angeles and started to play at the now defunct Ardmore Bridge Club. They had tournament bridge downstairs and money bridge upstairs. I played both, but mainly upstairs. However, once they discovered that I wasn't 21, they wouldn't let me play upstairs any longer.

They used to tell a story about the players at the Ardmore. The tournament players downstairs wanted nothing to do with the money players upstairs. They felt that money bridge was just a game of luck (not so), and tournament bridge was more skillful.

On the other hand, the rubber bridge players upstairs wanted even less to do with the tournament players downstairs. They felt that if a person wouldn't put up any money to back his skill, how good could he be?

And so it came to pass that they never spoke to each other. However, the restrooms were upstairs and the tournament players were forced to go upstairs from time to time thus coming in close contact with the despised money players.

One particular afternoon after the duplicate session was over, it seemed that everyone had to go upstairs at the same time. One of the players, the late Malvine Klausner, then one of the reigning queens of the tournament world, and a player who never played money bridge, was late getting up the stairs and ran into a full house in the Ladies' Room.

As this was an emergency she went into the Men's Room! When she finally resurfaced, one of her friends saw her emerging and asked her if she knew where she had been. Malvine admitted to knowing where she had been. "Well, was there anybody else in there?" "Yes," said Malvine, "there were a few guys, but they were only rubber bridge players."

After having been kicked out of the Ardmore Club, I tried playing at the Los Angeles Bridge Club. They let me alone so I had a new place to haunt.

There was a stretch of one year when I left my beloved "Los Angeles Bridge Club" to go into the Army. When I came back I found that practically everyone was at the very same table as when I left. Furthermore, many of them didn't even know I had been gone. Life goes on.

Still, my most memorable money bridge hand took place in my home town, Minneapolis, some 37 years ago.

On this particular afternoon only three of us, along with the owner's wife, Helen Winsten, were there. Although Helen was a good player, she didn't relish playing in this particular game, and besides, she was also the cook and had to be on call to make sandwiches, etc.

After much pleading she finally consented to play. We were playing Chicago for two cents a point (much more than I could afford), and it was the fourth deal and both sides were vulnerable with North the dealer.

Just as North was about to bid, in walked a local expert, Len Lazarus. Helen immediately asked him if he would take her hand so she could make sandwiches. We were all starving. Len agreed. This was the hand:

North dealer
Both sides vulnerable

```
                        North (Owen)
                        ♠ Q 7 6
                        ♡ A 7 6 4
                        ◇ Q 8 3 2
                        ♣ A Q
        West (me)                           East (Earl)
        ♠ K 8 2                             ♠ J 9 3
        ♡ —                                 ♡ K Q 10 9 2
        ◇ K 10 9 7                          ◇ 5 4
        ♣ 10 8 7 6 4 2                      ♣ 9 5 3
                        South (Len)
                        ♠ A 10 5 4
                        ♡ J 8 5 3
                        ◇ A J 6              Kitchen (Helen)
                        ♣ K J
```

I was playing with a friend, Earl Levinson, and North was the late Owen Rye, a wonderful player. This was the bidding:

West	North	East	South
—	1 ◇	pass	1 ♡
pass	2 ♡	pass	3 NT
pass	4 ♡	pass	pass
double	pass	pass	redouble
(all pass)			

In my younger days I hated to see anybody play an undoubled contract when I knew the trumps were breaking badly. Of course, I didn't expect a redouble, but my tuition was paid up for the next quarter, so how bad could it be?

I decided to lead my fourth best club. Len won in dummy with the ace and led a low diamond to the jack and my king. I exited with another low club.

Len won in his hand with the king and led a low heart to the ace, as I discarded a spade. Len nodded as if to reassure Owen things weren't all that bad. I was getting sick.

A low heart was led from dummy and Earl won the queen, cashed the king of hearts and exited with a low heart to Len's now bare jack. I discarded diamonds.

Keep in mind declarer no longer has any more trumps in either hand and Earl still has the last trump. Totally unnerved, declarer led a low spade towards the queen. I flew up with the king, cashed my four winning clubs and Earl's trump took the last trick. Down six, doubled and redoubled: 3400 points at two cents a point! Next quarter's tuition and then some. (Remember we are talking 35 years ago.)

You haven't forgotten about Helen in the kitchen, have you? Just as the hand ended she appeared triumphantly with four beautiful roast beef sandwiches as only she would make them. She then asked what happened on the last hand.

When Len told her the result there was a brief discussion (one hour), about who would pay for this debacle. I remember thinking to myself, "Please God, the biggest set of my life and I may not collect."

The Solomon-like decision was that they should each pay half. Helen always said those were the four most expensive roast beef sandwiches she had ever prepared.

The Bridge Professional as a Writer

In the early fifties "The Bridge World" magazine published the first bridge article I had ever written. I was going to the University of Minnesota at the time and I was ecstatic.

From there I began to write other articles. I ghosted some major syndicated bridge columns, and eventually started to write books! Me, books? It didn't seem possible. But people bought them and they are still buying them 20 books later. They have even been translated into other languages. This means that I can confuse people on three continents!

Presently I am a regular contributor to the three major bridge publications in this country—"The Bridge World," "Bridge Today" and the "American Contract Bridge League Bulletin." I am also dickering for my own syndicated column. They are not easy to come by, however.

One advantage to appearing in print is the mail I receive. Some players see me as a bridge doctor and they ask me to settle arguments. Husband and wife letters are not only the most frequent, but also the most acrimonious. One has to answer these letters with kid gloves.

I have two favorite correspondents. One is Walter Bingham, former Managing Editor of Sports Illustrated. Walter has an endless supply of "commuter train" stories for me. You see, he had this regular game every morning on the way to work. The players learned to time themselves and almost always finished before the last stop. In extreme cases they had been known to take an unfinished hand into the station and put the dummy on top of a garbage can lid in order to get a final result.

Once Walter became declarer in a difficult slam contract just as the train pulled in. Two of the players were in a hurry so the garbage can technique had to be scrapped. Walter suggested that everyone take his hand home and bring it back the next morning. Agreed. Then Walter was afraid that his partner, the least responsible player in the game, might forget to bring his hand back, so he offered to take it home himself. Agreed.

That night Walter laid out the two hands and studied the situation at length. Never has a declarer had more time to plan the play. The next morning Walter played the slam and went down one. Perhaps if he had had the whole weekend . . .

My other favorite letter writer is Gene Dillon, of Arizona. I know for a fact that Gene is a very good player and so is his wife, Bettie. They do quite well in tournament play, yet they have the most poignant things happen to them. To wit:

```
Dear Eddie,
    This is probably the last letter you'll get
from me unless you like to talk baseball. After
this hand from the Mesa Regional, I've decided
to quit bridge forever.


    West dealer              Neither side vulnerable

                        North
                        ♠ K 4
                        ♡ Q 10 8 7 6 5 3
                        ◇ —
                        ♣ A Q 7 4
        West (Gene)                 East (Bettie)
        ♠ J 10 7 5 3                ♠ A Q 9 2
        ♡ J 9 4                     ♡ 2
        ◇ A 7 5                     ◇ K Q J 9 8 6
        ♣ K 2                       ♣ J 3
                        South (Laughing Hyena)
                        ♠ 8 6
                        ♡ A K
                        ◇ 10 4 3 2
                        ♣ 10 9 8 6 5


    North started proceedings by opening one
heart, Bettie doubled and South made the odd
raise to two hearts. From that point on the
bidding escalated rapidly with Bettie and I
bidding spades and North bidding hearts and
more hearts. North finally bid six hearts which
I doubled.
    Then, South bid seven clubs! South had
thought that his partner had bid clubs some-
where along the line (he hadn't) and thought
that clubs would be better than hearts. I
doubled again, a little more loudly.
```

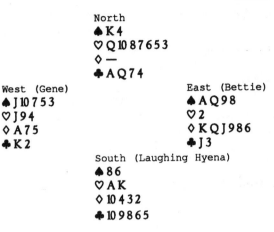

North
♠ K 4
♡ Q 10 8 7 6 5 3
◇ —
♣ A Q 7 4

West (Gene)
♠ J 10 7 5 3
♡ J 9 4
◇ A 7 5
♣ K 2

East (Bettie)
♠ A Q 9 8
♡ 2
◇ K Q J 9 8 6
♣ J 3

South (Laughing Hyena)
♠ 8 6
♡ A K
◇ 10 4 3 2
♣ 10 9 8 6 5

Now was the time for my "surprise" lead of the ace of diamonds, the unbid suit. Dummy ruffed, declarer entered his hand with the ace of hearts, finessed the queen of clubs, cashed the ace of clubs, and had no trouble taking the rest of the tricks. Seven clubs doubled—the suit being bid for the first time at the seven level—making. This resulted in a score that no one had ever heard of before: minus 1630.

You have probably noticed that my double of six hearts would not have fared so well either. This contract cannot be beaten with any lead, but at least everyone has heard of minus 1210.

Even with all that, everything would have been O.K. if declarer had not caused such a commotion by rolling on the floor in uncontrollable laughter.

> Your friend,
> Gene Dillon

Dear Gene,
Please don't give up the game. I need your letters for my articles.

> *Sincerely,*
> *Eddie Kantar*

The Bridge Professional as a Hired Gun

Bridge is a sport and as such is extremely competitive. Non-bridge players may have a hard time relating to this, but bridge players know.

As in other sports, everyone wants to win. However, since bridge is a game of skill, the same players dominate.

This domination has been broken up a bit by the appearance of the "sponsor" or the "customer." The sponsor is usually a wealthy person who hires a professional player as a partner. Or, he may hire an entire team of professionals.

As the sponsor is never as strong a player as the person (or team) that he hires, and as the rules state that each player must play at least 50% of the hands (in team play), some of the best players are not always winning any more.

At this point in time, about 80-90% of the top players play professionally. For the player the choice is simple—is he looking for glory or would he rather feed his family?

Why do these sponsors hire pros? There are at least three reasons: glory, master points, and the desire to play better.

I'm not sure whether glory or master points is first on the list, but I know learning to play better is definitely last.

Furthermore, once a person hires a professional player it is difficult to go back to one's regular partner. Imagine, if you will, being an average tennis player and suddenly being able to play a doubles set with Chris Evert or John McEnroe as your partner. How much fun do you think it is going to be to go back to your regular doubles game? You got it; it's going to be the pits. So what if you never got to hit the ball during a crucial point; you won, didn't you?

I have been playing professionally for more years than I would like to remember. However, I do it sparingly while others do it year round.

I make sure I play with people I like and who actually wish to improve their game. It makes me feel like I am doing something worthwhile.

One experience I had playing professionally many years ago still lingers. First, a little background.

The lady's name was Millie and we had never played together. She came to the table armed with at least two dozen old convention cards, her compact, her lunch, my lunch, her Turkish cigarettes, the newspaper, "People" magazine. Also, she was nervous.

In fact, she told me that the one thing that made her the most nervous was if the director was ever called to the table. I made a mental note. We were an East-West pair for the first session. It was quite clear that if Millie didn't clear the table we would never get started. One of the opponents complained and the director was called. The first visit.

At table two there was a revoke (Millie, of course) and the director was summoned.

At table three a card fell to the floor face up (guess whose) and back came the director to adjudicate. What do you think Millie's mental state was at this point?

At table four Millie undertrumped with the setting trick and they made an impossible contract. I was beginning to visualize the lowest score in contract bridge history—and I was getting paid.

Finally, we moved to the historic table number five. This was the first board. Millie was East and I was West.

North dealer
East-West vulnerable

```
                         North
                         ♠ A K 10 8
                         ♡ A J 10 2
                         ◇ 4 3 2
                         ♣ A K
         West (me)                         East (Millie)
         ♠ 7 6 5 3                         ♠ 2
         ♡ Q 8                             ♡ K 9 7 6 5 3
         ◇ K Q 8 7                         ◇ J 5
         ♣ 10 6 5                          ♣ Q 9 8 7
                         South
                         ♠ Q J 9 4
                         ♡ 4
                         ◇ A 10 9 6
                         ♣ J 4 3 2
```

West	North	East	South
—	1 ♡	pass	1 ♠
pass	4 ♠	(all pass)	

Millie and I were on defense, already a bad sign. I started with the king of diamonds and Millie played the jack. Declarer liked what he saw out there and won the ace. Great. I had already blown a trick on opening lead.

With the ten-nine of diamonds now poised to take a trick, declarer was in good shape and decided to draw a couple rounds of trumps ending in his own hand. Millie discarded a high heart on the second spade. Declarer then led his singleton heart to the ace and followed with a low heart from dummy. Millie played the king, of course, declarer ruffed, and my queen fell. Great. Now dummy's hearts were all good.

It never dawned on Millie that I must have the queen of hearts. (If declarer had it he would have finessed.)

Declarer stopped to consider his good fortune. First we had given him a trick in diamonds on opening lead and then we had set up his heart suit. And we were still going to be there for another hand. He couldn't contain a smile.

While all this happiness was taking place in the South seat, Millie was quite busy in the East seat. She had put her cards down and lit up one of her treasured long green Turkish cigarettes.

When play was ready to resume, Millie picked up all the cards she had already played, including the trump and her king of hearts. All the while her real hand was resting snugly on the table.

Declarer decided it was now time to draw the remaining trumps and he played a trump from his hand to dummy. Millie followed! Of course, I am paid to notice things like this, but I'm human too. All of the things Millie had done thus far had finally gotten to me, and I didn't see or say anything.

Well, declarer wasn't sure what was going on but he *knew* his hearts were good. He drew my last trump and played the jack of hearts. Millie was right there with the king.

It was easy enough to set up a suit against Millie and me, but it was impossible to use it!

The director was called for the fourth time in five rounds. Strangely, he was not too far away this time. He ruled that the "play had gotten out of hand" and awarded our opponents average-plus on the board.

Later, they appealed and were awarded a top score on the hand.

Millie plays much better these days. However, there are some other good stories the boys tell.

Did you hear the one about. . .?

My ill-fated T.V. show (1975).

I
Ex-Partners

Marshall Miles

Help!

BEFORE I TELL you about the following hand (played in a friendly, non-stake Team of Four game) you should be armed with a number of pertinent facts:

1. Marshall Miles is one of my very best friends.

2. He is usually a most discerning declarer, even though at times a little exotic.

3. He is addicted to making sensational leads if he feels the bidding calls for it.

4. He is often filled with admiration for an opponent who has hoodwinked him with a Miles-type-of-zany-brilliancy.

5. He stays over as a houseguest whenever he comes in from San Bernardino for the weekend.

6. He and Phyllis (my wife) get along very well and recently had two nice sessions playing the Mixed Pairs in the Nationals at Denver.

7. He has a theory about rebidding five-card majors after partner's non-forcing one notrump response. (Whenever Marshall has a broken two-loser suit such as: K-Q-10-9-x, A-J-10-9-x or K-J-10-9-x, he prefers to rebid the suit rather than pass with a minimum balanced hand.) This, of course, is counter to standard practice.

8. Marshall, a bachelor, is hopelessly attracted to wild, imaginative women. Particularly married ones.

Keep all this in mind as I am going to ask you to help me answer an important question later. But first this hand:

South dealer
Both sides vulnerable

                          North
                          ♠ 4
                          ♡ K 10 6
                          ◇ Q 10 6 5 4
                          ♣ A 9 8 7
        West   East
        ♠ A 3 2   ♠ Q 7 6 5
        ♡ 7 5 2   ♡ Q 8 4 3
        ◇ K 9   ◇ J 3 2
        ♣ K J 6 5 4   ♣ Q 10
                          South
                          ♠ K J 10 9 8
                          ♡ A J 9
                          ◇ A 8 7
                          ♣ 3 2

Phyllis		*Me*	*Marshall*
West	North	East	South
—	—	—	1 ♠
pass	1 NT	pass	2 ♠ *
(all pass)			

* The theory in action.

Phyllis, without a moment's hesitation, led the nine of diamonds! Marshall played dummy's ten and when I covered with
the jack, Marshall for some obscure reason misread the diamond
position. He thought that I had the K-J-x and Phyllis the 9-x. How
naive! In any event, he ducked my jack in an effort to cut com-
munications and avoid the impending diamond ruff.

Slightly upended by this turn of events I returned a diamond,
just to see what was going on. The diamond was ducked, and
when Phyllis won the king there was a strange look in Marshall's
eyes. He glanced to his left and gave Phyllis a long look. Was it
hate or admiration? At any rate, Phyllis returned a heart, covered
by the ten, queen and ace. Marshall tried the king of spades
which lost to the ace. He won the club return, entered his hand

via a heart and sneakily played his eight of spades. I won the queen. When I turned up with the odd diamond and Phyllis ruffed Marshall's ace, my worst fears were confirmed. . . Marshall was positively enthralled with Phyllis' opening lead. He didn't even mind being the only player this side of the Atlantic not to take a diamond trick with this holding . . . nor did he mind going down a trick, the only player in the room to achieve a minus score with the North-South cards.

Perhaps you have already guessed my question. In view of what I have told you about Marshall and in view of this opening lead, should I or should I not let him be our houseguest next weekend? *Help!*

Phyllis and I waiting for Marshall to show up.

Marshall and me—our younger days.

Slam Bidding

I REMEMBER WRITING somewhere that it was a good idea to open one notrump with a five-card major providing your major wasn't strong and you didn't have a weak doubleton on the side. The other night I picked up: ♠ 10 4 ♡ A K Q 6 5 ◇ K J 9 ♣ A 6 5.

Remembering what I had written, and figuring it might even be true, I opened the hand with one heart. My partner, Marshall Miles, responded two clubs and there I was struggling for a rebid.

Two hearts seemed like a gross underbid as did three clubs. I lacked a heart for a three heart rebid so I finally settled on two diamonds, which was at least forcing. This solicited two spades from Marshall and I now had to describe the strength of my hand.

As we play the two spade bid, the fourth suit, it might not even show a spade stopper let alone a suit, so I was not supposed to bid notrump unless I had a spade stopper. Furthermore, I had to show my extra values; so I leaped to four clubs, feeling a bit uneasy. (I had also written somewhere that when a player bids two suits and jumps in a third he has a singleton or void in the fourth suit.)

Now Marshall bid four notrump and after I dutifully showed my two aces he bid six diamonds! The tortured sequence up to this point was:

Me	Me	Marshall
♠ 10 4	1 ♡	2 ♣
♡ A K Q 6 5	2 ◊	2 ♠
◊ K J 9	4 ♣	4 NT
♣ A 6 5	5 ♡	6 ◊
	?	

Now what was to become of me with my three card diamond suit? I knew Marshall must have four diamonds and he could well have a singleton heart so my choices, it seemed to me, were either pass or six notrump. I passed. The opening lead was a spade and this was the entire deal:

```
                    North
                    ♠ A J
                    ♡ J 2
                    ◊ A Q 6 5
                    ♣ Q J 10 9 2
      West                            East
      ♠ Q 8 7 5 3                     ♠ K 9 6 2
      ♡ 7                             ♡ 10 9 8 4 3
      ◊ 8 7 3                         ◊ 10 4 2
      ♣ K 8 7 4                       ♣ 3
                    South
                    ♠ 10 4
                    ♡ A K Q 6 5
                    ◊ K J 9
                    ♣ A 6 5
```

I rose with the ace in dummy, drew trumps in three rounds and quickly discarded dummy's jack of spades on a good heart. Lacking a dummy entry, I simply played ace and a club, conceding a trick to the king, but making my slam.

The postmortem started as we began to criticize each other for winding up in our four-three diamond fit instead of our five-three club fit, or even better our five-two heart fit. Then it was noticed that six clubs can be defeated with a spade lead as West ruffs the second heart so that a spade cannot be discarded early. A spade lead also defeats six notrump and the five-one heart break defeats six hearts. The only makable slam is six diamonds. We finally decided that we had bid the hand beautifully.

My Phoenix Favorites

IF THE READER will indulge my skipping around from hands in the Phoenix Trials to hands in the Open and Team events and even to one hand from the rat races (side games), I will be able to relax and in my own disorganized way present my accumulations.

The betting odds, going into the Trials, were three to one that Marshall and I would wind up in at least one cue bid. For a while we were letting everybody down, but in the fourteenth round, against Hubbell and Nash, with both pairs all but eliminated from contention, the following gem was dealt, which hereafter will be referred to as the cue bid gambit.

South dealer
Both sides vulnerable

                        North
                        ♠ K Q J 7
                        ♡ J 10 5 4
                        ◊ 9
                        ♣ K 10 9 7

        West   East
        ♠ 5 4   ♠ A 3 2
        ♡ Q 7   ♡ 9 6 3
        ◊ A J 8 7 5 2   ◊ K 10
        ♣ Q 8 5   ♣ A J 6 3 2

                        South
                        ♠ 10 9 8 6
                        ♡ A K 8 2
                        ◊ Q 6 4 3
                        ♣ 4

Marshall		*Me*	
South	West	North	East
pass	pass	pass	1 ♣
double	redouble	pass	pass
1 ◊	double	2 ◊ !	(all pass)

Well, we had done it again. We had miraculously found our
worst contract. The worst. Even clubs plays one trick better. I
can't remember offhand whether Marshall took four or five tricks,
but I do remember that East, Hubbell, made the mistake of listening to our postmortem conversation as to whether my two diamond bid should be a cue bid or a natural bid. This was to prove
a fatal error for Hubbell, because just two deals later this hand
arrived on the scene:

West dealer
Both sides vulnerable

```
                         North
                         ♠ Q 10
                         ♡ J 6 5
                         ◇ Q 10 9 7 6
                         ♣ J 5 4
        West                              East
        ♠ K J 2                           ♠ 9 8 7 5
        ♡ A K 9 8 7                       ♡ Q 3 2
        ◇ K 2                             ◇ J
        ♣ A 9 7                           ♣ Q 8 6 3 2
                         South
                         ♠ A 6 4 3
                         ♡ 10 4
                         ◇ A 8 5 4 3
                         ♣ K 10
```

Marshall	Nash	Me	Hubbell
West	North	East	South
1 ♡	pass	1 NT[1]	2 ◇
double[2]	3 ◇	pass	3 ♠[3]
double[4]	pass	pass	pass[5]

[1] We play two hearts as an encouraging response.
[2] Thinking that I was short in hearts and the the opponents were in trouble.
[3] Things are getting better all the time.
[4] Is this really happening?
[5] Yes.

Do you see what happened? Hubbell, recalling our disaster, now thought that Nash was making some sort of a black suit cue bid. Nash thought that Hubbell had psyched diamonds and was afraid to go back.

Hubbell enjoyed playing this hand just about as much as Marshall enjoyed the other one. The only difference was that he was doubled. Our careful defense defeated the hand 800. Had we been a little more careless we might have gotten 1400.

The moral of that story is obviously not to listen to the opponents discussing their disasters.

There was a little excitement in the side game when big Jim Linhart (6'10") picked up the South hand:

South dealer
North-South vulnerable

```
                        North
                        ♠ A K J
                        ♡ Q 9 3
                        ◇ 9 8 7 4 3
                        ♣ K 9
      West                              East
      ♠ Q 7 6 5                         ♠ 9 8 4 3 2
      ♡ 2                               ♡ K 8 7 6 5
      ◇ —                               ◇ A 10
      ♣ Q J 8 7 6 5 3 2                 ♣ 10
                        South
                        ♠ 10
                        ♡ A J 10 4
                        ◇ K Q J 6 5 2
                        ♣ A 4
```

Linhart

South	West	North	East
1 ◇	pass	3 ◇	pass
3 ♡	4 NT (!)	5 ◇	5 ♠
6 ◇	6 ♠	pass	pass
7 ◇	huddle		double

It seems that East was getting a little nervous when West started to huddle over seven diamonds. Not only did East double out of turn, but he also placed his ace of diamonds face up on the table to relieve his partner of any further anxiety.

The director was called and the ruling was that West was barred from the bidding but that South still had a chance to bid and the ace of diamonds would be a penalty card, to be played at the first legal opportunity.

Linhart couldn't exactly see making seven diamonds with that trump ace staring him in the face, so he bid seven notrump, which ended the bidding.

A spade was led, and in the excitement Linhart finessed and the jack held. The nine of hearts held the second trick and then the queen of hearts and another heart finesse. East was merrily following to everything. Dummy was entered with a club and the two spades were played, East following. Linhart was getting desperate—he was running out of suits. His last chance was clubs, so he banged down the club ace. East wanted to discard a heart on the second club, but Linhart gently wrapped his arm around East and after a lengthy tug-of-war dislodged the ace of diamonds from his clutches. With that card out of action, Linhart picked up steam and actually made his contract. Bridge is a very simple game.

Another of my favorite "side game" stories stars Mrs. Bea Petterson. Second to speak, with none vulnerable, Bea gazes at this balanced minimum:

♠ A K Q 10 3 2 ♡ — ◇ — ♣ A K J 8 5 4 2.

She is somewhat perturbed to hear her right hand opponent open seven diamonds! Bea bid seven spades, which ended the bidding.

Dummy had a singleton spade and a doubleton small club and assorted red garbage. Bea ruffed the opening diamond lead, plunked down her high spades, gratefully noticing that the spade jack was doubleton, and then played the ace-king of clubs. When the club queen dropped doubleton, she claimed the balance.

As the East-West players were quietly—very quietly—putting their hands back in the board, Mrs. Petterson turned to her right hand opponent and said, "May I please see what a seven diamond opening bid looks like?"

"I opened one diamond," was the bitter reply.

Teaching at the El Cab Country Club in Encino, California.

Is This Game for Real?

I COLLECT BRIDGE HANDS. I even file them away under various titles in an old shoe box. Who knows? Some day they may come in handy.

Under the letter "J" I file hands that I entitle "joke hands." They really happened all right, but they struck my funnybone somewhere, and besides, I didn't know where else to put them.

The first exhibit comes from an early round in a National Mixed Pairs. As usual, I am fighting to qualify, and though I will name names in some of the hands, I cannot get myself to mention my partner's name here. Suffice to say that she is nervous and impressionable.

Even though it is an early round we are not doing too well. On the first board, the husband opened with one spade, and his wife passed. Upon viewing the dummy he exploded that they had missed a game—when would she ever learn to bid, etc., etc. However, once the bad breaks unfolded, it turned out that there was no game. Naturally they were the only pair not in it, and he made amends by complimenting her, etc., etc.

By this time I was a little upset, wondering why these things always happen to me, and my partner also knew that we had just gotten another zero. Then *this* happened. The line-up was: South, adoring husband; North, beaming wife; East, Nervous Nellie; West, me.

East dealer
North-South vulnerable

North
♠ A Q 9 7 5
♡ K 7
◇ 10 8 6 5 4
♣ 3

West
♠ 10 3
♡ 8 6 5
◇ A K J 9 7 3
♣ Q 10

East
♠ K 8 6 4
♡ A 3
◇ Q
♣ K J 9 7 6 2

South
♠ J 2
♡ Q J 10 9 4 2
◇ 2
♣ A 8 5 4

Me	*Beaming Wife*	*Nervous Nellie*	*Adoring Husband*
West	North	East	South
—	—	1 ♣	1 ♡
2 ◇	2 ♠	double	3 ♡
double	(all pass)		

First, let me explain that my partner has never made a penalty
double in the past unless they were down at least four. I, on the
other hand, never double unless they can make an overtrick.

I led the king of diamonds, and first dummy put down her
trumps. Next came South's monologue: "Darling, you have the
king of trumps! Thank you." Then came the spades, "Oh, sweet-
heart, the ace of spades! How nice." Rather than show her diamonds, Beaming Wife next put down her singleton club. "Oh,
you're kidding!" gushed South. "Not a singleton club too!" Now
North was definitely afraid to put down her diamonds, but, sens-
ing her fear, South said, "Don't worry, Honey, I don't have many
of those."

By this time I was wondering why they weren't in a slam, and
my partner would have been happy to concede two overtricks
just to get out of there.

Trying to retain my composure, I shifted to a trump at Trick two. My partner grabbed dummy's king and returned a trump. Declarer drew one more round of trumps and led the jack of spades. I played the ten, but to no avail. My partner was just too happy to take a trick, any trick, and she won the king.

My record was intact—my double had netted declarer an overtrick. My partner's record of never making the right play was also intact, and so we left for the next table. (If she ducks the spade we actually beat the hand.)

If Tobias Stone, by mistake, should happen to be reading this article—he says he doesn't read my stuff because I won't read his book—I want him to stop worrying about that hand he and Waldy von Zedtwitz defended against Marshall and me in San Francisco. It's too late, I'm going to tell:

Stoney (right) in Jackson, Mississippi, studies his cards. His partner on that occasion was Johnny Crawford. My partner, obviously confused by one of my bids, was Harold Guiver.

East dealer
East-West vulnerable

North
♠ J 7 4 3
♡ K Q 4
◇ K Q 8
♣ 7 4 3

West
♠ 8
♡ 10 7 6
◇ J 9 3 2
♣ K Q J 8 2

East
♠ A K 10 6 2
♡ 5 3
◇ 7 6
♣ A 10 6 5

South
♠ Q 9 5
♡ A J 9 8 2
◇ A 10 5 4
♣ 9

This was what some would jokingly call the bidding:

Von Zedtwitz	Me	Stone	Miles
West	North	East	South
—	—	pass [1]	1 ♡
pass	2 ◇ [2]	2 ♠	pass
pass	3 ♡	pass	4 ♡
(all pass)			

[1] Which is why I won't read Stone's books.

[2] Which is why he won't read my articles. I just don't believe in bidding one spade over one heart on a bad four-card suit. Stoney doesn't believe in bidding . . . period.

Waldy led the eight of spades to Stoney's king, Marshall false-carding with the nine. Trance number one. Then Stoney led the ace of clubs. Waldy, wanting a spade ruff, played the deuce of clubs. Stoney played the ace of spades; Miles dropped the queen.

Trance number two. Waldy was now afraid that Miles was out of spades and that a third spade from Stone would allow Miles to ruff high and later discard a club on the spade jack.

So Waldy ruffed the ace of spades and played the king of clubs!

Readers are left to conjecture who should have played what and when, and also as to the duration and decibel level of the postmortem that took place between East and West.

To put in a hand about Stone without mentioning Roth would be terribly unfair. Here is one from the Life Masters Men's Pairs in San Francisco, at that same 1965 Fall Nationals:

Alvin Roth, at the Mayfair Club in New York,
recalls the last time he played against Marshall and me.

North dealer
East-West vulnerable

                              North
                              ♠ Q 9 3
                              ♡ 7 6 4
                              ◊ 8 5
                              ♣ A J 10 6 3

          West   East
          ♠ A 7 2   ♠ J 8 6 5
          ♡ J 9 8   ♡ K 10 3 2
          ◊ K J 10 2   ◊ Q 9 7 3
          ♣ Q 7 2   ♣ K

                              South
                              ♠ K 10 4
                              ♡ A Q 5
                              ◊ A 6 4
                              ♣ 9 8 5 4

Roth	*Me*	*Dunn*	*Miles*
West	North	East	South
—	pass	pass	1 NT ·
(all pass)			

· Weak

Roth led the deuce of diamonds and Miles won the third
diamond, discarding a heart from dummy. Miles tried the nine of
clubs, and Roth played the queen. [Roth's play of the queen would
be right whenever his partner had K-x-x, and it would lose nothing if East had K-x—in fact the play might gain in that latter
event, since Miles might duck the queen and later finesse for the
king. The only time Roth's play loses is when East has the singleton king—a situation that Roth deemed "impossible" because of
East's pass.—E.B.K.] Dummy's ace and East's king comprised a
rather healthy looking trick . . . from my point of view, anyway.

At this point Roth shook his head sadly at his partner, Mike
Dunn, and said something to the effect that Mike had let him
down "again" and that the whole thing was hopeless.

Dunn, in the meantime, had already searched though his

spades to see whether he might have another club, and when he couldn't find one he just couldn't get himself to apologize for having been dealt the singleton king of clubs.

After the hand the mystery was cleared up. "There is no hand with a singleton club that doesn't balance over a weak notrump with a two club bid in the pass-out position!" came the words from Mount Olympus. Dunn fought back by mentioning something about the vulnerability and the weakness of his own hand, but all he got was a pitying look. *

Playing in an open pair game a few years back, I had this experience:

---

* In fairness to Al, here is an excerpt from his book, Bridge Is A Partnership Game (p.92):

You hold (nonvul vs. vul):

♠ K J x x	Opp	Part	Opp	You
♡ Q 10 x x	1 NT	P	P	?
◊ K 10 9 x				
♣ x				

2 ♣. This is also a take-out bid. You are too weak to double, but must take action. You have the advantage of being nonvulnerable and should find a landing spot.

South dealer
Both sides vulnerable

```
                        North
                        ♠ K 5
                        ♡ A 9 4 3
                        ◇ A K 8
                        ♣ K Q 7 5
        West (me)                       East
        ♠ 3                             ♠ 7 2
        ♡ J 8 6 5                       ♡ K Q 10 7
        ◇ J 9 2                         ◇ Q 6 4
        ♣ A J 9 6 4                     ♣ 10 8 3 2
                        South
                        ♠ A Q J 10 9 8 6 4
                        ♡ 2
                        ◇ 10 7 5 3
                        ♣ —
```

The bidding, with East-West silent:

South	North
2♠[1]	4NT[2]
5◇[3]	5NT[4]
6♣[5]	6NT[6]
7♠[7]	

[1] Strong.
[2] Loud.
[3] Soft.
[4] You're kidding!
[5] No king.
[6] I don't believe we're off an ace, but what can I do?
[7] This hand doesn't look right for six notrump.

Smugly, I laid down the ace of clubs, and when North saw that card she gave birth right at the table. In a voice that can't be described here, she said to South, "Don't you think I know what I'm doing?" South ruffed, drew trumps and claimed, saying in the same tone of voice, "And don't you think I know what I'm doing?"

However, misfortune can befall anyone. Witness how carefully Lew Mathe played the following hand in three clubs:

```
                        North
                        ♠ K J 8 7 6
                        ♡ A J 9 2
                        ◊ 9 3
                        ♣ 4 2
West                                    East
♠ A 10 5 4                              ♠ 9 3
♡ K Q 8 7 6                             ♡ 10 5 3
◊ 10 6 5                                ◊ K J 8 2
♣ 3                                     ♣ A K 10 5
                        South
                        ♠ Q 2
                        ♡ 4
                        ◊ A Q 7 4
                        ♣ Q J 9 8 7 6
```

Lew, sitting South in a rubber game, opened three clubs with a 40 part-score, and played it there.

West led a high heart which Mathe won in dummy. A diamond was led to the queen, followed by the ace of diamonds, under which East dropped the king.

A third diamond was led and Mathe carefully—very carefully—ruffed with dummy's four. A heart was ruffed back to the closed hand, followed by a fourth round of diamonds.

West was pleased to be able to put his singleton three of trumps to work, and this turned out to be the setting trick!

If Mathe carelessly ruffs the third round of diamonds with the deuce, he makes the hand. You can't win 'em all.

We will now end up with one of my favorites, although it took me two weeks to recover from the trauma. This was played at rubber bridge, with North-South vulnerable and 40 on score:

East dealer
North-South vulnerable

```
                        North
                        ♠ A Q 5
                        ♡ A K 10 2
                        ◇ 3
                        ♣ K J 9 6 5
        West                              East
        ♠ 8 7 6 3 2                       ♠ K J 10 4
        ♡ J 8 4                           ♡ 5
        ◇ 10 5 2                          ◇ A K 4
        ♣ 10 3                            ♣ A Q 8 7 4
                        South
                        ♠ 9
                        ♡ Q 9 7 6 3
                        ◇ Q J 9 8 7 6
                        ♣ 2
```

West	North	East (me)	South
—	—	1 ♣	pass
pass	double	redouble	4 ◇ (!)
(all pass)			

I was East, and afraid to double four diamonds for fear my partner might bid four hearts.

West led the ten of clubs, and down came the dummy. South was furious. The nerve of his partner doubling one club with a singleton diamond! On and on South ranted. Finally he subsided and apologized, asking us not to pay any attention to his comments. (This, of course, is like hitting a man over the head with a sledge hammer and telling him to overlook the pain.)

Anyway, I won the queen of clubs and decided to base my defense on the hope that my partner had either J-x or 10-x-x of trumps, in which case constant club plays would build up the setting trick for us in the trump suit.

I returned the seven of clubs at Trick 2, and declarer discarded a heart, winning the club in dummy with the nine. A diamond was led from dummy. I took the ace and my partner discarded the four of hearts!

I said, "Irving"—his name was Irving—"no diamonds?" Irving admitted to having a diamond and the four of hearts became a penalty card.

Clearly, it would do me no good to return a club at this point, because my partner would have to play that four of hearts anyway. Another brilliancy struck: I decided to return my singleton heart. Now, when I got in with my king of trumps, I could give my partner his club overruff and in turn ruff a heart myself.

I led my five of hearts. Declarer played low and my partner played the eight. Another exposed card! He had forgotten that he had to play the four which was lying on the table.

Declarer now came back to his hand via a spade ruff, knocked out my other high diamond, and made his contract. I never did give Irving that club overruff.

Two weeks later Irving came up to tell me that it was actually my fault that he had defended as he had. He had gone home that night and thought about what was going on in his mind at the time of the debacle.

It turned out that when I played my ace of diamonds the first time the suit was led, Irving automatically placed declarer with the king. Irving knew I was going to return a club, and he thought that declarer would ruff high with his probable K-Q-J of trumps, and that he (Irving) would discard a heart . . . which he did.

If I had won the first diamond with the king, he would not have been one trick ahead of himself, and so the whole hand was my fault. Of course.

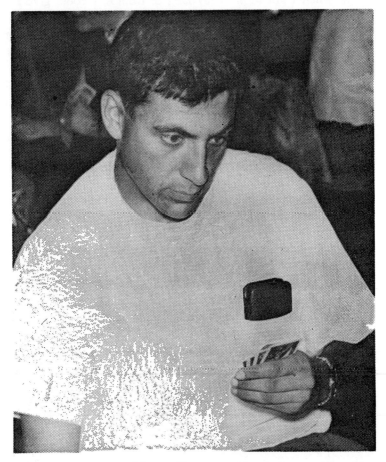

Me, a million years ago.

Down 4000 Points!

SPEAKING OF RECORDS. On the first day of regular play at the Summer Nationals in Boston a few years ago, one pair achieved a score of plus 3070 points on a single deal!

The following day the Daily Bulletin came out with a prediction that plus or minus 3070 would certainly be the biggest score any one pair would make on any one deal during the entire tournament.

What the Bulletin overlooked was that the following day the Mixed Pairs was to be held. No logical predictions can be made until that event is over.

East dealer
North-South vulnerable

```
                        North
                        ♠ 9 8 4 2
                        ♡ 8 3 2
                        ◇ J 7 6
                        ♣ A Q 2
        West                            East
        ♠ 6                             ♠ A K J 7 5
        ♡ K J 10 9 5                    ♡ 7
        ◇ 9 5 3                         ◇ A K Q 10 8 4 2
        ♣ J 8 7 3                       ♣ —
                        South
                        ♠ Q 10 3
                        ♡ A Q 6 4
                        ◇ —
                        ♣ K 10 9 6 5 4
```

East opened with a forcing club and South conceived the bid of two diamonds! Surely this overcall would produce some fireworks. West bid a peaceful two hearts, but when North raised to three diamonds East chanced a double.

South promptly redoubled for rescue but North didn't get the message and passed! East decided that three diamonds redoubled suited him fine so he passed also. West led his singleton spade.

Now for some good news and some bad news. The good news was that the defenders failed to find their spade ruff. The bad news was that even with this gift declarer went down seven tricks for a loss of 4000 points.

More good news and bad news. The good news: North-South set a new minus record that did hold up for the remainder of the tournament. The bad news: Neither North nor South seemed to appreciate what they had accomplished.

Partnerships have been known to break up over a single hand; even one bid or one errant play may do the trick. The next hand is an example of this in action, and I'm involved.

Playing with my frequent partner, Marshall Miles, is at times trying. For example, he has devised a "super method" for responding to a two notrump opening bid. The method is so complicated that bridge playing math professors at both UCLA and USC have thrown up their hands in despair when the method was explained. But I am expected to play it, come what may.

Just to give you an insight into this method (it's really quite good if your first name is Albert), a raise to three notrump is a transfer to four clubs.

In order to really raise to three notrump you must bid three spades! Imagine agreeing to play a method where a raise from two notrump to three notrump shows clubs.

In any event we were using this method at the last National Championships in Lancaster, Pennsylvania. Fortunately, both Marshall and I are poor card holders so neither one of us opened two notrump until he hung one on me on the last day of a ten-day tournament.

By that time I couldn't even remember the normal responses to two notrump let alone the all encompassing Milesian responses.

In any case, this was the hand that proved beyond a shadow of a doubt that honesty is the best policy.

South dealer
Both sides vulnerable

North (me)
♠ Q 4
♡ 7 6
◊ A J 10 7 6 3 2
♣ 5 4

(East-West hands immaterial)

South (the Master)
♠ A K 9 3
♡ A K 4
◊ K 8 5
♣ K 7 3

Marshall opened two notrump with the South cards, never once looking up to see whether I was going to remember the responses or not. Using "the" method my proper response, the Master informed me later, was four diamonds, a slam try in diamonds. Well, who would have thought that diamonds meant diamonds, so that bid never even entered my mind.

North (me)
♠ Q 4
♡ 7 6
◊ A J 10 7 6 3 2
♣ 5 4

South (the Master)
♠ A K 9 3
♡ A K 4
◊ K 8 5
♣ K 7 3

I naively thought that slam was remote and our best chance for a good tournament score was to play in three notrump. So I bid it! Keep in mind the Master now thinks I have made a transfer to clubs, a slam try.

East passed and Marshall, according to the rules, alerted the opponents that I had just made a transfer to four clubs. I swear I did not close my eyes, look up in utter horror, or begin to sweat noticeably. I was too worried about how I was going to convince the Master that I really had diamonds and three notrump was one huge super airball, when lo and behold, the Master announced to the whole table, "It is supposed to show clubs, but I don't believe it, pass!"

Well, I could have jumped across the table and kissed Marshall. He had actually figured out that I had forgotten his beloved convention. What a player.

As the play started I realized that something had gone awry. There were twelve sure notrump tricks with the diamonds behaving. We had missed a cold slam.

That scoundrel Miles had passed my transfer and we didn't get to our cold slam.

"Marshall," I said, "the least you can do is honor my transfer bids. What do you think—I don't know what I am doing?"

Strange, Marshall has never asked me to play with him again, and here I am the only person in the world other than the Master who knows how to respond to two notrump properly.

II
Ex-Partners

Robert Hamman

Compression Plays

WEBSTER'S DEFINES "COMPRESS" as *to press together; to force, urge or drive into smaller compass; to condense.* So what does this have to do with contract bridge?

In the game of contract bridge we are sometimes forced to let our partner play an occasional hand. Often our partner will play four spades, for example, with 10 top tricks. After considerable effort on his part he will come up with nine. Not so bad. Actually what he has done is to compress the hand by only one trick. A one trick or single compression is to be expected from most partners and it was just as much our fault for not giving him (her) a little extra leeway.

Problems do arise, however, when partners have a two or three trick leeway and still manage to come home lame. We are now in the dangerous area of "multiple compression." Partners who regularly perform multiple compression plays have to be treated with singular care. The most popular cure is to allow them to bid only clubs and diamonds—and diamonds not too often.

One would think that only weaker players are guilty of compression plays. On the contrary, some of the best have been guilty and at some of the most embarrassing moments.

Let me lead off with the man who invented the expression "compression play," Bob Hamman. He has the lovable habit of reminding all his partners of their most flagrant compression exhibits, and reminding them at just the right psychological moment.

Can you imagine the pleasure we all received when Hamman played the following hand on VuGraph vs. the Dallas Aces in a three corner match including Los Angeles and Omar Sharif's Circus? (At that time Hamman was not a member of the Aces.)

```
                    North
                    ♠ —
                    ♡ J 10 8 2
                    ◇ 7 6 3
                    ♣ A 10 8 7 4 3
West                                    East
♠ 10 9 2                                ♠ J 8 5 4 3
♡ Q 7 6 5                               ♡ 9 3
◇ A K 5 4                               ◇ 9 8 2
♣ J 2                                   ♣ Q 9 5
                    South
                    ♠ A K Q 7 6
                    ♡ A K 4
                    ◇ Q J 10
                    ♣ K 6
```

It was in this match, I believe, that Hamman requested to sit South for column purposes. The translation of this is that he is sure to do something brilliant that either I or someone else will want to use in a column or article. It will be so much easier for us if he sits South so we won't have to do any hand rearranging. Sweet lovable Bob.

On this hand, he played in three notrump sitting South, naturally, against the opening lead of the king of diamonds and a shift to the jack of clubs.

The line of play selected by our hero was to win the king of clubs and play the ace, king, queen and a small spade. East won the eight and jack, and exited with a diamond to West's ace. West played a second club and when West turned up with the queen of hearts, Hamman's partner (me) became the victim of a single compression play.

The fact is that Hamman both lost the spade spots and miscounted his tricks. He thought he needed four spade tricks. The intricate play of winning the king of clubs and playing ace-king and a third heart would have insured nine tricks against anything short of a forest fire.

A favorite fall pastime is compressing slams . . . or even grand slams!

After bidding the following hand to seven diamonds in some fifteen minutes, Marshall Miles managed to compress the play in fifteen seconds. (Incidentally, all of the people you meet in this article are good sports, but if by some chance I should run into foul play, let it be known that the prime suspects can be found here.)

East dealer
North-South vulnerable

North
♠ 10 4
♡ A K Q 3 2
◊ K Q 10
♣ A K 4

South
♠ A K 7 6
♡ J 4
◊ A J 3 2
♣ J 7 6

Just to give you a chance for a little compression of your own, how would you play seven diamonds after West leads a trump and East has shown a weak black two-suiter in the bidding? (East follows to the first trump play.)

Solution:
You should play off two high trumps from dummy. If all follow, you have 13 tricks if hearts break; or, if they don't, you should have a simple black suit squeeze on East.

If, however, East shows out on the second trump, you must cash your four black suit winners, hope you can cash four heart tricks, and cross-ruff the balance. The trap is not to ruff a spade prematurely as West with a 2-4-5-2 distribution can discard a club.

Ira Rubin managed to compress a four heart contract in the World Championship on the same hand that his counterpart bid and made six hearts.

```
                        North
                        ♠ A
                        ♡ A
                        ◇ A K 10 7 6 3
                        ♣ 8 7 6 4 2
        West                                East
        ♠ 8 7 5 4 2                         ♠ K J 10 3
        ♡ 4 3                               ♡ J 5 2
        ◇ J 9 8 2                           ◇ Q
        ♣ A K                               ♣ Q J 10 5 3
                        South
                        ♠ Q 9 6
                        ♡ K Q 10 9 8 7 6
                        ◇ 5 4
                        ♣ 9
```

Rubin got a spade lead and cashed the ace and king of diamonds . . . oops, not quite. East ruffed the diamond and returned a trump and Rubin had to lose two more spades and a club.

In the other room, Chiaradia, playing six hearts for Italy, received the lead of the ace and king of clubs. He entered dummy with a trump and cashed the ace of diamonds. When East played the queen, Chiaradia, a trusting soul, decided to believe. He ruffed a club back to his hand, drew trumps and finessed the ten of diamonds. A diamond was ruffed and the ace of spades was the reentry to the diamonds.

Rubin could have insured his contract by simply cashing the ace of hearts and playing a club at trick three. He now would be able to win the diamond return in dummy and ruff himself back to hand with a club to pull trump and take his ten top tricks.

Another factor in slam compression is nervousness. Give a player a choice of too many finesses and he is apt to go plum berserk.

How nervous are you?

North
♠ J 7
♡ A 7 6 5
◊ A Q 10 2
♣ A 10 9

South
♠ A K 10 4 3 2
♡ K 2
◊ K 5
♣ J 3 2

Assume you are playing six spades with the opening lead of the four of clubs. What would your compression avoidance play be?

Solution:
Your best shot to avoid compressing this one is to rise with the club ace and lead a spade to your ace. Assuming the queen has not fallen, you should enter dummy with the ace of hearts and lead the jack of spades. This is merely to tempt a cover. If the jack is not covered, rise with the king and if the queen does not fall, cash the king of diamonds and finesse the ten in an effort to rid yourself of both losing clubs.

Take full compression marks if you finessed either the club at trick one or the spade later on.

This is a hand that was destined for compression:

North
♠ A 10
♡ K 6 5
◊ A K 9 7
♣ Q 10 8 7

West
♠ J 4 3
♡ A 9 7 4 3
◊ Q 10 6 5 4
♣ —

East
♠ 9
♡ Q 10 8
◊ J 8 3 2
♣ K 6 5 4 3

South
♠ K Q 8 7 6 5 2
♡ J 2
◊ —
♣ A J 9 2

This hand came up in the Open Pairs a few years ago at Bridge Week. Most declarers played six spades. When West led the ace and another heart, declarer had little option but to win the king, play two rounds of trump ending in dummy, discard two clubs on the top diamonds and take a club finesse. West invariably discarded his last trump on this and declarer was one down.

It was at the tables that a diamond was led that true compression reared its ugly head. Declarer gleefully won the diamond, discarding a heart, played two spades ending in dummy, and discarded the last heart on the diamond. Now, if declarer simply wishes to make his slam, he ruffs a heart back to his hand, draws the last trump and concedes a club. How many declarers do you think did that? Right. Not one.

After playing two rounds of trump and ridding themselves of both hearts, the temptation to make seven was just too great. The queen of clubs was led from dummy and ducked around to West, who once again discarded a trump, played a red suit, and forced South to concede the setting trick to the king of clubs.

My friend, Harvey Cohen, submits the following ˙quadruple compression play˝ as a possible record.

East dealer
Both sides vulnerable

> North
> ♠ J 7 6
> ♡ 5 3
> ◊ 8 7 5
> ♣ A 10 8 7 6
>
> South
> ♠ A Q 10 9 5
> ♡ J 9
> ◊ K J 4
> ♣ K Q J

West	North	East	South
—	—	1 ◊	1 ♠
pass	2 ♠	pass	2 NT
pass	3 ♠	pass	4 ♠
double	(all pass)		

Opening lead: ◊ 9

Before reading further, how would you play this hand after East wins the ace of diamonds and returns a diamond to your jack, West producing the deuce?

Cohen mused about what West might have for his double at this point. Surely he must have the king of spades and a heart honor, reasoned Cohen. If this is true and I sneak a small spade past West, I can take my spade ace and then play on clubs. If West has three or four clubs along with his three spades to the king I will discard a heart or two and make a few columns. He made a few columns. You see, this was the entire deal:

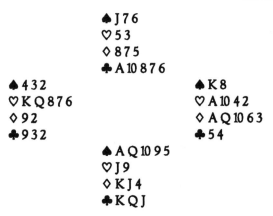

East won the king of spades and gave West a diamond ruff. The defense then collected two heart tricks, putting Cohen down 500. Had Cohen simply played to the ace of clubs and finessed the queen of spades, the ace would catch the king, and now two more clubs are cashed. Dummy is entered with the jack of spades and both hearts go off on the clubs. Making six!

Truly a magnificent compression play.

Before I am deluged with law suits and examples of my own compression plays dating back to year one, I offer two recent exhibits.

```
                  North
                  ♠ 7 6
                  ♡ J 5 4
                  ◊ A K 9 8 4 3
                  ♣ J 10
West                                East
♠ K Q J                             ♠ 10 9 8 5 4 3 2
♡ 6 2                               ♡ Q 10 8
◊ J 10 2                            ◊ 6
♣ K 9 7 4 3                         ♣ A 2
                  South
                  ♠ A
                  ♡ A K 9 7 3
                  ◊ Q 7 5
                  ♣ Q 8 6 5
```

Sitting South, for the column of course, I opened one heart and became declarer in four hearts with no adverse bidding. (When they see I am going to be the declarer they seldom sacrifice.)

West led the king of spades which I won. I cashed the ace of hearts and studiously made the "book safety play" of a low heart to guard against four hearts to the queen-ten in either hand. Unfortunately, as they say, trumps broke 3-2. East won the queen of hearts and played the ace and another club to West, who returned a third club giving East a ruff, to complete my compression play.

For my second number I show you a hand that rivals Cohen's for multiple compression:

South dealer
Both sides vulnerable

```
                     North
                     ♠ A 6 4
                     ♡ J 7 5
                     ◇ K 9 5 4
                     ♣ 10 9 5
      West                           East
      ♠ K J 10 5 2                   ♠ 9 3
      ♡ 3                            ♡ K Q 10 8 6
      ◇ Q 8 7                        ◇ 6 3
      ♣ Q J 7 2                      ♣ K 8 4 3
                     South
                     ♠ Q 8 7
                     ♡ A 9 4 2
                     ◇ A J 10 2
                     ♣ A 6
```

South	West	North	East
1 NT˙	pass	2 NT	(all pass)

˙16-18

I cheated a point and opened one notrump with fifteen.

```
                    ♠ A 6 4
                    ♡ J 7 5
                    ◊ K 9 5 4
                    ♣ 10 9 5
♠ K J 10 5 2                            ♠ 9 3
♡ 3                                     ♡ K Q 10 8 6
◊ Q 8 7                                 ◊ 6 3
♣ Q J 7 2                               ♣ K 8 4 3
                    ♠ Q 8 7
                    ♡ A 9 4 2
                    ◊ A J 10 2
                    ♣ A 6
```

Again they led the right suit against me, a small club. East put up the king and I won the ace. Feigning strength in clubs and spinelessly trying to avoid the diamond guess, I returned a club. This worked like a charm . . . in reverse. West won the jack and East played the eight, which I thought might be suit preference for spades. West played two more clubs and I cleverly threw off a diamond from dummy, partially blocking that suit, and a spade and a heart from my hand.

When West shifted to a heart and East played the ten, I wanted to go back and open one diamond. I ducked the heart. East now shifted to the nine of spades. Would this torture ever cease? I tried the queen but I knew the king would be placed on top of her immediately. It was. Fearing that if I ducked this another heart would come back I finally took the ace. At this point I saw my partner check our convention card to see whether or not he had forgotten that we were actually playing weak notrumps.

Now I came to life and led the king of diamonds and finessed the jack of diamonds smack into West who calmly produced four more spade tricks. Not losing my cool I kept the ace of hearts in my hand and the nine of diamonds in dummy to insure taking the last trick. I did. Down four. As my partner (sweet lovable Bob) pointed out, I had started with five tricks in aces and kings. If I had just cashed out, which is what he would prefer I do in the future on any hand where compression is possible . . . which means any hand I play, I would only have gone down three.

God Save Our Country

THE PHONE RANG. "Hamman speaking." "Yes Robert, what can I do for you?" "First, I want to apologize for all the nasty things I've ever said about those exotic bidding sequences that you and Marshall use, and second, I want you to play a hand for me."

The man who was soon to represent our country in Italy in the World Championships then called off the following hand which took place at the office in Los Angeles. (The "office" is the L.A. Bridge Club, so termed in order to add a little respectability to our wayward lives.)

North
♠ A 10 9 x x
♡ 10 x x
◇ —
♣ A J x x x

South
♠ Q J x x x
♡ J x x
◇ x x x
♣ x x

"So how do you play this hand with a low diamond out?"

"Just a minute, " I said, "what's the contract?"

"Guess," said Bob.

"Four spades?" — "No."

"Six spades?" — "No."

"Five spades?" — "No."

"Spades??" — "No."

"Five clubs?" — "No."

"*Clubs??*" — "No."

"Four hearts?" — "No."

"Three notrump?" — "You're getting warmer."

I just couldn't stand it any longer, and exploded, "Please, Bob, just tell me the contract!"

"THREE DIAMONDS DOUBLED, WHAT ELSE!" Bob roared.

"You must be joking," I gasped. "Was this for money?"

"Yes."

"Your own money?"

"Sure my own money"

"Who were you?"

"North."

"And who was South?"

"Paul Soloway."

"How'd the bidding go?"

"Very logically."

Neither side vulnerable

	Robert		*Paul*
West	North	East	South
—	—	1 ◇	pass
1 ♡	2 NT [1]	pass	pass [2]
double	3 ♣ [3]	pass	pass [4]
double	pass	pass	3 ◇ [5]
double	pass [6]	pass	pass [7]

The bidding as explained by Hamman:

[1] My two notrump bids are for the other two suits when the opponents have bid two suits.

[2] Soloway plays the two notrump overcall for the minors even if one of the minor suits has been bid.

[3] Two notrump doubled did not appeal to me.

[4] If we get doubled I'll run to my longer minor. I hope Hamman isn't worrying about me interpreting his two notrump overcall. After all, I've been around.

[5] Might as well play in our longest suit.

[6] Might as well . . . he must have at least seven diamonds.

[7] Won't Bob be proud of me. Too bad I'm not strong enough to redouble and teach these jokers a lesson.

"So what finally happened," I asked, not in the mood to play three diamonds doubled on these cards.

"The story has a happy ending," Bob said. "The opponents could have beat us eight, but they beat us only seven. They slopped a trick."

"Forgive my asking, but are you really going to Italy?"

"Sure. You know I am."

"God save our country!"

Rio de Janeiro, 1969. Hamman and me in the Bermuda Bowl losing to the Italians, Walter Avarelli (sitting to my left) and Giorgio Belladonna. Kibitzing Robert was our team captain, Oswald Jacoby.

A Tale of Two Partners
I. Norman

THE FOLLOWING STORIES are about my two most recent partners.

Since everyone who plays bridge is familiar with Robert (Bob Hamman), let me begin by telling you a bit about Norman (Norm Cressy).

Norman began playing bridge in college about 25 years ago and then more or less gave up the game. He got himself a Ph.D. in chemistry, taught at the college level and then decided to sack academia and teach tennis. I met him a couple of years ago through a mutual friend and have been playing tennis with him ever since.

I soon discovered Norman is a class A mathematician, so I installed him as my "lines of play" consultant. Whenever I come across a hand that I plan to write up in quiz form that has two or more lines of play that seem to be close percentage-wise, I give Norman the problem. First, I work it out using my own primitive tools, and then I check with the master to see whether I'm right.

My jottings usually cover about a quarter of a sheet of regular paper. Norman always returns about three full sheets of complicated equations with the percentages neatly circled at the bottom of the last page. Incredibly, we agree most of the time. However, his work is ever so much more impressive—also accurate to the decimal point.

Working on these bridge problems revitalized Norman's interest in the game. He finally decided he wanted to become a good player. Fine. That was the good news. The bad news was the way he set about it.

He started reading the most advanced books on the game, works on squeezes and other complicated endings—all this before knowing which bids are forcing and whether a double is negative, penalty or takeout. (He alerts *all* doubles).

Norman bids as if the bidding will never get back to him again. He never passes an invitational bid (we might decide to use them as slam tries in the future), and he goes for a home run on every hand. This *does* make for a rather exciting evening.

Until now his sister, Gloria Levy, a Life Master, sacrificed herself occasionally to play duplicate with Norman. But after Norman worked endlessly with my forehand volley (my nickname is "One Millimeter," indicating the distance I can stretch to hit a forehand volley), guilt feelings set in; so now Norman and I play together—occasionally. One session with Norman requires about four days for recovery.

Recently there was a Swiss Teams event at the Wild Whist Bridge Club in Los Angeles. The top eight qualifiers were to play in a Knockout the following three days—but only if they affixed a star on their entry blank.

Our team, Gloria and Lou (Gloria's husband, Lou Levy, is a bona fide expert), Norman and I and Susan Ross. Susan was our fifth in case we actually made it into the Knockouts. Incidentally, Susan *is* a knockout.

I told Norman before we started that it would be helpful if he learned how to give count on defense. He said he would like to learn. So the afternoon of the event I gave Norman a signaling lesson complete with follow-up test.

Norman passed with flying colors. He has a great memory, and if he can make a chart he never forgets anything.

We were going to play four matches, and Norman and I were stuck with each other, so to speak, for all four.

Now I want to make sure you get the picture. Norman was determined to be a good partner, not to go for a touchdown on every play and to give perfect count on defense.

How did this all work out? You be the judge. We did lose our first match because our partners had their only soft game of the evening. How did Norman do?

Not too bad. He only passed out of turn once and gave me perfect count in this situation:

                    North (dummy)
                    ♡ A 10
West   East (Norman)
♡ Q 8 7 4 3   ♡ J 9 2
                    South
                    ♡ K 6 5

I led the heart four against a spade contract. When dummy played the ten, Norman produced the deuce, showing me an odd number.

Things got better in subsequent matches. Overlooking his false claim, we also had this:

                    North (dummy)
                    ♣ A 10 8 2
West   East (Norman)
♣ 5   ♣ K 9 7 4 3
                    South
                    ♣ Q J 6

We were defending three notrump with four defensive tricks already in, and declarer ran the club queen. You guessed it—Norman was right there with the three, giving me perfect count!

Nevertheless, our partners were very good in the last three matches and we won them all. We were in the Knockouts!

The following morning I received a telephone call from the Whist asking me who this Cressy was. Was he some ringer from the Cavendish in New York? (We're still laughing over that one.)

No, I assured them, he was no ringer from the Cavendish. Just a good tennis-playing friend of mine. "How many master points does he have?" "As many as he won last night plus about two."

You see there is something I didn't tell you about Norman. He bids and plays with consummate confidence. He looks for all the world as if he knows exactly what he is doing, and one day soon he will.

Our team won its first Knockout match (I played with Susan) by one IMP! We were now in the semifinals and Susan couldn't play the next night. I had to play with Norman again—with only one day's rest.

We got off to a flying start on the very first board when my LHO responded three diamonds (transfer) to an opening two notrump bid with: ♠ 2 ♡ 7 6 4 3 ◊ 7 5 2 ♣ 10 9 7 5 3.

He then passed his partner's three heart bid.

His partner had: ♠ A K 4 ♡ A 2 ◊ Q 6 4 ♣ A K J 4 2.

Down four. Unlucky.

Then this hand came up:

West dealer
North-South vulnerable

```
                        North
                        ♠ 7 6 4 3
                        ♡ K 7 4 3
                        ◊ A J
                        ♣ Q 6 5
        West                              East
        ♠ A Q 10 9 8                      ♠ —
        ♡ 6 5 2                           ♡ Q J 9
        ◊ 10 6 5                          ◊ K 9 7 2
        ♣ 10 3                            ♣ K J 9 8 7 2
                        South
                        ♠ K J 5 2
                        ♡ A 10 8
                        ◊ Q 8 4 3
                        ♣ A 4
```

	Norman		Me
West	North	East	South
2 ♠ [1]	Dbl [2]	pass	3 NT
(all pass)			

[1] Weak Two
[2] "How else could I show you my ten points?"

So there I was in three notrump. I won the spade ten with the jack, East shedding a middlish club. Then I led a diamond to the jack which held, East pausing momentarily. Next I led a low heart from dummy. East decided to duck! I guess he was hoping his partner had the ten and would be able to get in to lead a club. In any case my ten held the trick.

Even with all this I couldn't see nine tricks. I tested the hearts. They broke. I discarded a spade on the fourth heart, East discarded a club and West a spade. I cashed the diamond ace, entered my hand with the club ace and exited with the *queen* of diamonds. East was able to score his K-9 of diamonds, but then had to surrender the ninth trick to dummy's club queen after cashing the king. Silence around the table.

No more would they look at Norman's dummies with a smile on their face and a gleam in their eye. At half-time the match was close. As I recall, we were down about six IMPs.

Then Norman picked up, vulnerable:

♠ J 8 6 4 ♡ A 10 3 ◇ 2 ♣ A 10 7 5 3.

He heard an opening one diamond bid to his right so naturally he doubled. "How else could I show you my nine points?"

I responded one heart and the opener now bid one notrump. Norman bid two clubs, of course. "How else could I show you my suit?"

I corrected to two hearts holding:

♠ A 7 2 ♡ Q 8 5 2 ◇ K 7 6 4 3 ♣ 2.

Everyone passed and I received the favorable lead of the spade king. By this time everyone was a bit more prepared for the dummy. It was slowly dawning on me that I no longer could judge the value of my hand in view of Norman's bidding. Oh well.

Even though I made two hearts we lost the match. Four members of our team felt bad about this loss. One pretended to feel bad.

Let me conclude this section with my latest telephone conversation with Norman:

Me: "So you played bridge last night. Any interesting hands?"

Norman: "Yes, one very interesting one."

Me: "Tell me."

Norman: "Well, I opened with a double."

Me: "And what were you showing your partner this time?"

Norman: "I don't know. They redoubled."

Norman gets a bit excited occasionally, but in the end he will be a good player. You watch.

A Tale of Two Partners
II. Robert

A WEEK OR TWO LATER I was on my way to Reno to play in a couple of events with Robert (Bob Hamman). We had decided in a moment of mutual weakness that it might be fun to play together again.

Our agenda was the Swiss Teams and the two-session Open Pairs the following day.

Before sitting down to play I had to review "Robert's Rules" that all Robert partners are supposed to live by.

1. If a number of bids are available and one of them is three notrump, that's the bid.

2. Never play Robert for the perfect hand. He never has it.

3. If everyone at the table seems to be bidding their head off, trust them, not Robert.

4. When contemplating a slam, always subtract a king from what it sounds like Robert has before bidding the slam.

5. Be practical.

6. Do the right thing.

Well, I thought, I can do anything for two days. After all, hadn't I just finished an event with Norman?

Problems arose immediately. No mention was made about what to do when there's a conflict in the rules!

With neither side vulnerable in the Swiss, I picked up the following hand: ♠ Q 7 4 ♡ A Q 6 ◊ A J 10 5 ♣ 9 6 4.

The bidding:

Me		*Robert*	
South	West	North	East
1 ◊	pass	2 ♣ ¹	double
pass	2 ♠	3 ♣ ²	pass
?			

¹ Shows 13 cards with some clubs.
² Same 13 cards with a few more clubs.

Clearly I was in trouble. Rule 1 definitely told me to bid three notrump. But Rules 2 and 3 warned me away. Rule 5 had me in a quandary, and of course, one is always haunted by Rule 6. I bid three notrump.

A small spade was led and this was the dummy:
♠ 5 ♡ 8 4 3 2 ◊ 7 4 ♣ A Q J 10 5 2.

The ace-king of spades were to my right and the club finesse worked. Rules 1 and 6 proved to be the winners in this case. But how long could I keep this up? Not long.

Soon I picked up: ♠ Q 5 3 ♡ A 7 3 ◊ A K 10 ♣ 8 6 3 2.

Robert opened one spade and the bidding developed:

Robert	Me
1 ♠	2 NT
3 ♡	3 ♠
4 ♡	?

At least I could eliminate Rule 1. Rules 2 and 4 definitely warned me away form a slam. I couldn't adjust to Rule 5, and I couldn't live with Rule 6.

I ventured into the cold with the delicate cue bid of five diamonds. This was met with five spades which I passed. The opening lead was the ominous king of clubs.

These were the two hands:

Robert's Rules (repeated for convenience)

1. If a number of bids are available and one of them is three notrump, that's the bid.

2. Never play Robert for the perfect hand. He never has it.

3. If everyone at the table seems to be bidding their head off, trust them, not Robert.

4. When contemplating a slam, always subtract a king from what it sounds like Robert has before bidding the slam.

5. Be practical.

6. Do the right thing.

North
♠ Q 5 3
♡ A 7 3
♢ A K 10
♣ 8 6 3 2

South
♠ A K 7 4 2
♡ K 10 6 5 2
♢ —
♣ Q 9 4

East had the jack-ten doubleton of clubs and ruffed the third round. The eight of clubs and the ace-king of diamonds afforded parking places for the hearts so we went down only one.

I had broken Rules 2 and 4 and now I prepared myself to pay for it. It wasn't long in coming. "Edwin," (fundamental bidding lectures always start with Edwin), "if you hadn't refused to play Jacoby Two-Notrump, you would have had room to bid this hand and could have started with two diamonds. Then we could have avoided this trap." What could I say?

Incidentally, you may have noticed that some of the time I am North and some of the time South. This is done only for your convenience. Robert always sits South for column purposes. As he told me many years ago, sooner or later he is sure to do something brilliant and it will be easier when I write it up not to have to rearrange the positions.

That also wasn't long in coming.

East dealer
East-West vulnerable

                        North
                        ♠ A
                        ♡ K 4 3 2
                        ◊ A 7 6 5 2
                        ♣ A K Q

West   East
♠ Q J 9 8 5   ♠ 7 4 3 2
♡ A Q 10 6 5   ♡ 7
◊ K Q   ◊ J 10 9 4 3
♣ 10   ♣ J 7 3

                        South
                        ♠ K 10 6
                        ♡ J 9 8
                        ◊ 8
                        ♣ 9 8 6 5 4 2

	Robert		*Me*
East	South	West	North
pass	pass	1 ♠	double
2 ♠	3 ♣ [1]	3 ♠	4 ♠
pass	5 ♣	(all pass)	

[1] Shows 13 cards.

Opening lead: ♠ Q

Robert started by cashing the diamond ace and ruffing a diamond. This was followed by two rounds of clubs and another
diamond ruff. A heart was led toward the king. If West wins, he
is endplayed in either major, so he ducked. After winning the
king of hearts, yet another diamond was ruffed. Then the spade
king was cashed, the ten of spades ruffed with dummy's last
trump, and the last diamond ruffed with Robert's last trump. That
all comes to 11 tricks and a very neatly played hand.

In fact things were going rather well in the team game. We
had won our first four matches and in the evening we gave up
exactly nine IMPs in four matches. But it wasn't good enough.

We lost one match 6-2 when I misdefended two notrump. "Good field, no hit," said Robert.

The pair game is best left forgotten. On the very first board we (and I use this pronoun *very* loosely) let them make a vulnerable three hearts doubled. And that was one of our better boards.

And finally, when things could get no worse, I invented the following slam double to do nothing more than torture Robert, who, as I have been reading, has had a little trouble leading against slams lately.

This was Robert's (West) hand:

♠ 10 5 ♡ J 7 4 ◇ J 10 6 4 ♣ K 7 4 3.

The bidding proceeded as follows, with Robert sitting West.

Robert		*Me*	
West	North	East	South
—	pass	pass	1 ♠
pass	3 ♠	pass	4 NT
pass	5 ◇	pass	5 NT
pass	6 ♣	pass	6 ♠
pass	pass	double	(all pass)

What do you lead?

Robert reasoned as follows: If Eddie wanted a diamond lead he would have doubled five diamonds. If he wanted a club lead he would have doubled six clubs. If he wanted a heart lead he would have passed.

There were only three possibilities:

I. This is one of those rare slam doubles that calls for a trump lead.

II. This is a takeout double.

III. I am playing with an idiot.

As he told me later there was no conflict—they *all* applied. He finally led a diamond, and they made seven. This was the entire hand:

North
♠ 8 4 3
♡ Q 10 6 2
◊ —
♣ A 10 9 8 6 5

West
♠ 10 5
♡ J 7 4
◊ J 10 6 4
♣ K 7 4 3

East
♠ J 9 7
♡ K 9 8 5 3
◊ K 9 8 3 2
♣ —

South
♠ A K Q 6 2
♡ A
◊ A Q 7 5
♣ Q J 2

Possibility III was right—I should have doubled six clubs. At the time I thought they might redouble or perhaps even bid seven spades. Not such good thinking. If South were going to bid seven he surely would not bother to asks for kings and then bid it when he didn't find any. As for redoubling six clubs, well, it just never happens that way. I had forgotten Rule 5. I had blown Rule 6. Worse, I had become a III on Robert's list.

Robert's Rules (repeated for convenience)

1. If a number of bids are available and one of them is three notrump, that's the bid.

2. Never play Robert for the perfect hand. He never has it.

3. If everyone at the table seems to be bidding their head off, trust them, not Robert.

4. When contemplating a slam, always subtract a king from what it sounds like Robert has before bidding the slam.

5. Be practical.

6. Do the right thing.

III
Ex-Partners

Billy Eisenberg

Just Billy and Me — No Slam Intended

LET ME BEGIN by saying I have always had trouble with slam bidding with all my regular partners—including Marshall Miles and Bob Hamman. Although most of our disasters were (obviously) not my fault, neither of them agreed with my unbiased critiques of the auction. Ah, well . . . what can you expect?

Now I have another partner, Billy Eisenberg. He was reared on the East Coast where everyone is born playing five-card majors, forcing one notrump responses, and forcing sequences until all eternity, so I anticipated a few problems. Be that as it may, we tried to hack out a system combining his love of everything forcing with my opposite whims. The fact that he agreed to play four-card majors was no minor concession. However I notice that when the chips are down he still opens his beloved one diamond when he holds diamonds and hearts.

In return for his playing four-card majors, I practically had to give up my soul. For example, he recently forced this one upon me: one spade-two clubs; two notrump-three clubs is now forcing to four clubs. True, we play that the two notrump rebid shows extras and I have had to bolster up my two club responses. We have a whole list of sequences that are forcing to four clubs or four diamonds. God save us when we're dealt a hand that can take only nine tricks!

One other thing before getting to the hands. We have a fairly complicated system which we are not afraid to change with each bad result. Needless to say, we have changed the system so many times that we actually think we are winning when we remember what all the bids mean. Besides, we have some "obscure agreements." Some of our biggest problems have come from this area, as each player is sure that he alone has the memory of an elephant. Since I do most of the writing, I look at "the system" more than Billy does, so I should remember it better. He says the only way he can remember it is if I make up quizzes for him. Sure.

We were invited to play in the annual IMP pairs tournament in Mexico City. Last year we didn't do too well and, worse, we had to listen to Hamman cackle after he and Bobby Wolff won the event. This year we were determined to do better. After all, didn't we know the system perfectly?

This event began with a pro-am pair game. I drew a strong partner who got a bit ambitious on the following hand:

Me	Senor Ambicioso
♠ A K 9 7 5	♠ Q 10 8
♡ 5 3	♡ A K 9 7
◊ 6 4	◊ A K Q 5
♣ A 8 7 6	♣ J 5

After opening one spade, I found myself playing seven spades against the opening lead of the club king.

I immediately thought of the first hand in the best bridge book I have ever read, "Right Through the Pack" by Robert Darvas. The title of the story is "A Miraculous Grand Slam," where this guy has to make this impossible grand slam playing with the girl he loves or else she won't marry him. Was there any hope? I spotted something. If one player had precisely the Q-J-10 of hearts with precisely two trumps, and the opening leader had the K-Q of clubs along with at least four diamonds, I could effect a squeeze. The play would go:

Ace, king and ruff a heart, establishing the heart nine; ace and queen of spades; discard a club on the heart nine; return to my hand with dummy's last trump and run my trumps squeezing my left hand opponent. Fame, newspaper columns, and glory all danced before me.

At trick two I led a heart to the ace. No honor fell. My grand slam was doomed. The best I could do was apologize and play a club from dummy in order to ruff a club and hold it to down one. Even that didn't work. The opening leader started with ♠ J-6-4-3.

You may find this hard to believe, but that was one of the better slams I found myself playing in Mexico City.

The real tournament consisted of a series of fifteen nine-board matches, and the competition was fairly strong. Hamman-Wolff had returned. Peter Weichsel-Alan Sontag had arrived as well as Eric Kokish-Peter Nagy, Gaylor Kasle-Garey Hayden and Mike Moss-Marvin Rosenblatt.

We breezed along, winning our first five matches, when we finally met up with Kokish-Nagy. Things were going fine until I picked up this on the last hand of the match:

♠ A K J ♡ A K 4 ◇ J 7 3 ♣ A 10 5 4.

I opened two notrump. Billy looked at the ceiling. Uh-oh. He responded four spades. In our system four spades used to be a transfer to five clubs, later it was for the minors and now it had evolved into a mild slam try showing six spades and four hearts. Did he remember? Did I? Could anybody? What could I do?

My major suits made me think it was unlikely he was showing six spades and four hearts, but if he had remembered, maybe we had a slam. But what if he thought it was just to play? I passed four spades. The opening leader held ♠ 10-9-8-6-5-3. Partner's hand:

♠ 3 ♡ 10 6 ◇ A 9 8 6 2 ♣ K Q 8 6 3.

Billy took the obvious six tricks and there we were, down four. Fortunately, the rest of our game was solid, so we won the match 14-6 to find ourselves in a dogfight for first place with Hamman-Wolff.

Did I tell you we play Key Card Blackwood? We can show both the king and queen of trumps with our responses. Sounds good, doesn't it? Actually it has worked reasonably well on hands where we both knew which was the "agreed suit." We have three pages of notes on how to determine the agreed suit in complicated auctions. To us a complicated auction is whenever either player bids more than one suit. Now for the exhibit:

```
Billy                              Me
♠ K 5                              ♠ 10 8 6 4
♡ A Q J 10 7 5 4 3                 ♡ K 6
◇ 3                                ◇ K 10 6 4
♣ A 5                              ♣ K J 6
```

Billy didn't think he was strong enough to open two clubs so he opened one heart. I thought I was too strong to respond one notrump (he cannot have four spades as we play Flannery) so I bid one spade. In our system a one spade response usually shows four good spades or a five-card suit. Encouraged by my spade bid, Billy did something I have pleaded with him over the years not to do with me—jump shift in a short suit. He rebid three clubs. "Well," I thought, "my hand is looking better all the time; I think I will bide my time with a waiting bid of three diamonds." This was greeted by four hearts.

Before I considered the consequences of my next act, I launched into trusty Key Card. Billy's response was five spades, showing two of the five aces (king of trumps included) and the trump queen. Lovely. So we had the queen of trumps and I had perpetrated another abomination. What could I do? I raised to six hearts. After all, I didn't have to play the hand. He went down one.

None of these disasters was lost on Billy. He noticed that he always seemed to be declarer. The time had come for revenge.

A few boards later as West I picked up:

♠ A 5 ♡ K Q J 6 5 3 ◇ K 5 ♣ A K 7.

With only our side vulnerable the bidding proceeded:

Me		*Billy*	
West	North	East	South
2 ♣	pass	2 ◇	2 ♠
3 ♡	pass	4 ◇	pass
4 ♡	pass	5 ♡	pass
?			

Should I accept this invitation? Did it merely ask about spades? Well, we needed the points, so I bid six hearts. This was passed out and partner put down: ♠ J 6 ♡ 8 7 4 ◇ A 10 8 6 4 ♣ Q 5 3.

A top-looking spade was led and I quickly assessed my

chances. Not good. But there were two slight hopes. Number one: if the queen-jack of diamonds were doubleton with the singleton ace of hearts, I could play three rounds of diamonds and shed my spade. Number two: if the queen and jack of diamonds did not drop, I could always hope that the opening leader had a singleton spade and the heart ace, in which case I might be able to set up the diamonds.

Actually, it was a very unlucky hand. The queen-jack of diamonds were not doubleton, and South did not have eight spades, so I went down in another slam.

Undaunted after having been blitzed, we stormed back in our next match with a great result on this deal:

West (Me)	East (Billy)
♠ J 9 7 5	♠ Q 10 6
♡ A K J 5	♡ 6 4
◊ A Q 9 7	◊ 8 6
♣ 3	♣ A 9 8 6 4 2

Now I realize I should have saved this hand for last, because those few readers who have had sympathy for my impeccable bidding up to this point will surely throw up their hands in horror after this one.

The problem as I see it, with hands of this nature, is which suit to open. I am well aware that the five-card majorites snicker at such an easy problem and open one diamond. Others have come out in print saying one heart is best. However, they don't play Flannery and don't have to worry about partner skipping over a four-card spade suit.

My feeling has been to bid both majors and forget the diamonds. True, my spades are supposed to be better, but maybe just this once . . . . I opened one spade. Billy raised to two spades. Well, I didn't want to give up on a possible five-four or four-four heart fit, so I bid a natural three hearts. "Alert," screamed Billy.

"What is it?" he was asked.

"It shows a singleton heart with at least five spades," he said.

Well, after he bid four spades, it occurred to me that our opponents would never recover from this explanation. Sure enough, the opening lead was a small heart. I won the first trick with my "singleton jack," discarded a diamond from dummy on the third heart and crossruffed for ten tricks. Strangely, we were the only pair in this beautiful contract. When will the rest of the world learn to bid?

Actually, rebids of three clubs and three diamonds show singletons, but three hearts is natural. Are you impressed?

Alan and Peter were interested in our notrump structure as both Billy and I talk a good system. After the following hand they stopped asking.

West	East
♠ K Q	♠ A J 7 5
♡ J 9 8 6 4	♡ A 3
◇ A Q J 6 4	◇ K 10 9 3
♣ 10	♣ K 8 5

Me		*Billy*	
West	North	East	South
—	—	1 NT	pass
2 ◇	pass	2 ♡	pass
3 ◇	pass	3 ♠	pass
4 ♣	double	6 ◇	(all pass)

Two diamonds was Jacoby and three diamonds was forcing, showing five-five. Three spades showed a concentration in spades with diamond support, and four clubs was a mini cue bid. (What would you call it?) After the double Billy might have passed, but he thought I had the heart king and the slam was cold. In fact, he would have been right had my left hand opponent not led the ace of clubs and continued with the queen. Once again I was in a beautiful slam. All I needed was for my left hand opponent to have the A-Q-J-9 of clubs along with either the king-queen or any five hearts. He didn't—down again.

Somehow we survived all these disasters. Going into the last round we were in second place, two victory points ahead of Peter and Alan, and about eight or nine behind Hamman and Wolff, who, by trying to sit on their big lead of a few matches before, had very little left to sit on.

Clearly this was an important match for us, and we sat down to play some serious bridge. We had lost only three matches, all to lower-placed teams. Things started out well—that is to say we had no misunderstandings on the first two boards because we weren't in the bidding. Then this happened:

```
                        North
                        ♠ K 9 7 5 3
                        ♡ 9 8 6
                        ♢ 2
                        ♣ 10 7 5 3
    West (Billy)                        East (me)
    ♠ 6 4 2                             ♠ J 10 8
    ♡ Q 7 5 3                           ♡ K 2
    ♢ K Q J 7 5                         ♢ 10 9 6 4
    ♣ 2                                 ♣ K Q 9 8
                        South
                        ♠ A Q
                        ♡ A J 10 4
                        ♢ A 8 3
                        ♣ A J 6 4
```

South opened two notrump and North bid three hearts, transfer. South bid three notrump. This was alerted and explained as showing two of the top three spade honors with at least three spades. Everyone passed.

Billy led the king of diamonds. Looks pretty bad for the declarer, doesn't it? No way. No possible way. What could possibly go wrong? Besides, they were vulnerable.

Declarer won the third diamond, and I was left with the diamond four and Billy with the seven-five. South played the ace-queen of spades, upon which Billy carefully played the six-four to show me heart strength. We play a very careful game, you know.

At this point Peter, from one table away, asked Billy a question as declarer led the heart ten from his hand. Billy, thinking the third spade was about to be played, followed with the spade two! An exposed card! I won the heart king and in my misery did not realize that I was involved in a "Kantar for the Defense" position. I decided that if declarer had something like:

♠ A Q   ♡ A Q J 10   ♢ A 8 3   ♣ A J 6 4,

I could return the king of clubs and everything would be okay, as there would be no way of forcing Billy to play that spade. Remember, we had three tricks in at this point.

                          North
                          ♠ K 9 7 5 3
                          ♡ 9 8 6
                          ◇ 2
                          ♣ 10 7 5 3

West (Billy)   East (me)
♠ 6 4 2   ♠ J 10 8
♡ Q 7 5 3   ♡ K 2
◇ K Q J 7 5   ◇ 10 9 6 4
♣ 2   ♣ K Q 9 8

                          South
                          ♠ A Q
                          ♡ A J 10 4
                          ◇ A 8 3
                          ♣ A J 6 4

Alas, that was not declarer's hand. When I returned the club king, declarer won and played a low heart. Billy had to win the queen or else declarer would be in dummy. Then he had to play that cursed spade and declarer made three notrump. To say that a mild depression had settled over the table when the forced spade was played would be a major understatement. The feeling after the hand was over was so bad that even the kibitzers had to leave (to tell everybody what happened).

Then it dawned on Billy—the whole thing was my fault! If I had returned a diamond when I was in with the king of hearts, Billy would win and return a spade and declarer cannot come to nine tricks. [Declarer could have made me lead a spade when I was in with the king of hearts; but he would have come to the same eight tricks.]

I was stunned. I couldn't believe it. This whole mess was somehow going to be on my head? Then he uttered the fatal words—"didn't you see how I played my spades?" Yes, Billy, I saw *exactly* how you played your spades.

Well, in spite of this, we were going pretty good. Then came the last hand of the tournament. With both sides vulnerable, in third seat I picked up:

♠ A K 8 5 4 3 ♡ A 5 4 ◊ J 10 ♣ K 5.

The bidding proceeded:

	Billy		*Me*
West	North	East	South
—	pass	pass	1 ♠
2 ♡	3 ◊	4 ♡	4 ♠
pass	5 ♡	pass	?

Is this really happening again? Another slam invitation from the mad inviter? What should I do now? Well, I haven't turned down one of these yet. Six sp . . . double on my left, all pass. The opening lead was the king of hearts and this was the dummy for my last slam of the tournament:

♠ 96 ♡ — ◊ A K Q 9 5 4 3 ♣ 10 6 4 3.

Wonderful . . . if the Q-J-10 of spades was doubleton I would be cold for seven. I ruffed and ducked a spade into my left hand opponent, who quickly cashed the club ace. Down one.

We still beat Alan and Peter by one victory point for second place, and were within an eyelash of overtaking Hamman-Wolff. Somehow they managed to stop at four spades on this obvious slam hand. Had they bid as imaginatively as we, or had we bid as poorly as they, we would have won and they would have been second or third. But no, now we all have to listen to Hamman cackle for another year.

Bermuda Bowl, Manila, 1977. We won! Left to right: Coach Steve Altman, Bobby Wolff (half-hidden), me, Billy, Captain Roger Stern, Paul Soloway, John Swanson (the tall one), WBF President Jaime Ortiz-Patino, and, of course, Robert.

Eccentric Hands

HAVING JUST RETURNED from the Nationals in Hawaii, a number of hands are fresh in my mind.

Exhibit I

This is from our Vanderbilt match against the Martel team. I played with Billy Eisenberg against Kyle Larsen and Ron Von Der Porten. We were using bidding boxes for this match, which becomes important as you will see.

South dealer
Both sides vulnerable

	North	
	♠ A 9 8 2	
	♡ A	
	◇ A J 9 8 2	
	♣ Q J 8	

West		East
♠ K J 3		♠ 10 5 4
♡ Q 10 9 4		♡ J 8 5 3 2
◇ 10 5 4		◇ Q 7 6
♣ K 10 4		♣ 7 2

	South	
	♠ Q 7 6	
	♡ K 7 6	
	◇ K 3	
	♣ A 9 6 5 3	

Me	*Ron*	*Billy*	*Kyle*
South	East	North	East
1 ♣	pass	1 ◇	pass
1 ♠ !¹	pass	2 ♡	pass
2 NT	pass	3 ♠	pass
3 NT	pass	4 ♣ ²	pass
4 ◇ ³	pass	4 ♠	(all pass)

¹ Reached for my "1 NT" card but "1 ♠" popped out. Had I known
my rights, I could have replaced the one spade card with one
notrump. Instead I said, "Oh," and left the one spade card on the
table.
² Went to talk to the director before bidding four clubs.
³ Told Billy when he came back from the director not to make any
bid that would send us to a committee. (It takes forever, and you
always lose your appeal anyway.)

Opening lead: ♡ 10

This was not one of my happier moments in Hawaii. I could see at a glance that three notrump was almost surely cold, and that I hadn't the foggiest idea of how to play this contract.

Suddenly, I remembered something I once told a girlfriend. "When you don't know what to do, play your longest suit."

I ran the queen of clubs to the king, and West immediately returned the club ten, East playing high-low.

It seemed to me that Larsen, seeing a trump entry, was planning to give his partner a club ruff. In order to see a trump entry he probably had the king-jack of spades. It was all I had to go on.

I won the club return in dummy and led a low spade to the seven and jack. West returned a club, which East ruffed, but that was the last trick for the defense. I won the heart return in my hand and plunked down the queen of spades, trapping the now lone ten in the East hand. What does this teach us? (one of Billy's favorite questions). It teaches us two things:

(1) It helps to know the rules of the game;
(2) It helps even more to be lucky.

Exhibit II

My second Hawaiian entry shows me in action, demonstrating what I have learned from playing in partnership with Marshall Miles. In a team game with both sides vulnerable, I picked up in the South seat: ♠ 6 5 ♡ A K Q J 9 5 2 ◇ A 7 ♣ 10 3.

East	South
1 ◇	?

If I remember correctly, Marshall used to overcall three notrump with these hands and sit out the double. I tried three notrump! Nobody doubled and these were the hands:

```
                        North
                        ♠ K J 9 2
                        ♡ 8 7 6 3
                        ◇ 8 6 2
                        ♣ 6 5
        West                            East
        ♠ 10 8 7                        ♠ A Q 4 3
        ♡ 4                             ♡ 10
        ◇ J 5 3                         ◇ K Q 10 9 4
        ♣ A K J 9 4 2                   ♣ Q 8 7
                        South
                        ♠ 6 5
                        ♡ A K Q J 9 5 2
                        ◇ A 7
                        ♣ 10 3
```

West started out by cashing six rounds of clubs and shifted mercilessly to a spade. The defenders cashed two spades before I was able to claim down four.

This turned out to be a good result! At the other table our opponents sacrificed in five hearts against a cold five diamonds. They went down 800! Thanks, Marshall.

Exhibit III

Billy and I were playing in a strong home game practicing for Hawaii when the hostess mentioned that she had been reading about some of the crazy things that had happened in some of the home games I play in. She wondered if this was the home game I was referring to. "No," I said, "those things happen when I play with friends who are not experts. This is my strong game."

Relieved, she decided to kibitz. This was the next hand, I swear:

South dealer
Both sides vulnerable

```
                        North
                        ♠ A 10 6 4 3
                        ♡ K 7 4
                        ♢ 7 6
                        ♣ A 9 5
        West                            East
        ♠ Q 8                           ♠ J 9 5
        ♡ A 6                           ♡ Q J 5
        ♢ K 10 5 3 2                    ♢ J 9 4
        ♣ 10 7 6 2                      ♣ K Q 8 3
                        South
                        ♠ K 7 2
                        ♡ 10 9 8 3 2
                        ♢ A Q 8
                        ♣ J 4
```

Billy		*Me*	
South	West	North	East
pass	pass	1 ♠	pass
2 ♡	pass	3 ♡ !	pass
4 ♡	(all pass)		

Opening lead: ♣ 2

Give me a chance to explain. Billy and I were no longer
playing weak two-bids in hearts. I was afraid he had a good
playing hand with six hearts, and therefore overbid by raising.
Billy's bidding is also a touch aggressive. In any case, after the
opening lead I stopped to look at Billy's hand on the way to the
Oreo cookies in the kitchen.

"Billy," I said, "I'm sorry I bid so much." "That's okay," said Billy,
"we deserve each other." With that I left to eat the cookies.

When I came back, I asked how many he had gone down. He
said he had made it! "But that's impossible; what happened?"

This is what happened: East won the club lead and continued
with a club honor, which was taken in dummy. A club was ruffed
back to the closed hand and the ten of hearts passed to East.

However, East thought he saw the *king* of hearts played from dummy, and played low. Now four hearts is unbeatable, as Billy can hold his trump losers to one as well as set up the spades for diamond discards. "This is the strong game?" asked the hostess as she left never to return.

Exhibit IV

And now a true story of two friends of some years. Initials are going to be used to protect both parties.

The story begins in Los Angeles some twenty years ago at the Los Angeles Bridge Club. BK and AB are partners and have 60 on. Both sides are vulnerable and this was the first of the two infamous hands:

West (BK)	East (AB)
♠ A 10 6 5 4	♠ Q 3
♡ A Q 10 4	♡ K J 3
◇ A K	◇ J 6 5
♣ J 3	♣ A Q 8 7 2
1 ♠	2 ♣
3 ♡	4 ♡
4 NT	5 ◇
5 NT	6 ◇
6 ♡	pass

With the spade loser and the king of clubs offside, to go along with some bad breaks in the red suits, the hand was defeated two tricks.

West was furious that East raised to four hearts, even though he himself had jumped to three hearts over score. (Many play that a jump shift over score is forcing to what would be game with no partscore.)

Now comes the next hand and East-West still have that cursed 60 partial.

West (BK)	East (AB)
♠ K J 6 4	♠ A Q 2
♡ K Q 10 9 8 2	♡ 5 4 3
◊ A	◊ 7 6
♣ K 3	♣ A Q 8 6 2
1 ♡	2 ♣
2 ♡ !	pass

A diamond was led and when West saw the dummy he was livid. Sure that the partnership had missed a slam, he threw his cards face up on the table hurling insults left and right.

First he accused AB of making a lousy four hearts slam try on the first hand, and now he said that AB had dogged the bidding on this one.

At this point North interjected, saying that a cold slam was not missed and flashed the ace-jack-small of hearts.

Still the torrent from West continued. Some of it was even directed at the owner of the club who wasn't even in the game.

That night BK's account was settled and he was barred from the club. BK and AB ceased to speak to each other.

Two years later BK and his family moved to Australia for seven years and then on to England where they live now.

Twelve years have passed since the incident and one day AB walks into the Bridge Club and is given a telephone number to call. He calls.

He hears BK's voice on the other end. BK says, "I have decided to forgive you for making that slam try in hearts," these, his first words, after twelve years of silence.

The friendship was renewed and AB and BK had dinner with BK's family and they even had a social bridge game afterwards.

Why do I feel like I have just written an article for the National Enquirer?

Exhibit V

Let me end with a story that Jackson Stanley told me some time ago. I co-authored a book with Jackson, "Gamesman Bridge," and in the course of time he told me some wonderful stories.

At the time, Jack was sitting South playing duplicate against two loud-mouth college students. Jack's partner opened one club and the next hand overcalled two hearts. Jack waited for an alert, but nothing came. Finally, Jack asked fourth hand the meaning of his partner's two heart bid.

Before fourth hand could speak, the two heart bidder blurted out that it was a weak jump overcall. With that Jackson doubled. Again no alert from Jackson's partner. Finally, fourth hand asked Jackson's partner about the meaning of the double. Before Jackson's partner could answer, Jackson said, "we play penalty doubles over weak jump overcalls." Touche'.

The Best Hands of a World Olympiad
(and a few of the worst, too)

MY ENTHUSIASM for writing up a bridge tournament is directly proportional to how well my partner and/or team fared in the tournament. I had to drag myself to the typewriter for this article.

The tournament, THE V WORLD PAIR OLYMPIAD, was held at the Hyatt Regency Hotel in New Orleans, June 17-30, with 47 countries represented.

The opening event was a 10-session pair game with cuts after the fourth and sixth sessions—everyone starting from scratch for the final four sessions.

My partner, Billy Eisenberg, and I were among the top ten pairs until the last four sessions. After the first final, or seventh session, we were dead last!

After the eighth session, when we were still dead last, a few eyebrows were raised. After the ninth session we still had a death grip on last place, and were definitely walking the other way whenever we saw anybody we knew.

Before the last session we made a vow to get ourselves out of this mess. We played our hardest and were rewarded. We finished 38th, made enemies for life of the two pairs that finished beneath us, and walked out of the room with our heads high, mentally resolving never to play another pair game with each other.

What follows are some of my jottings from the Pair Game.

How would you play this trump suit (spades) in a slam contract with no adverse bidding?

Declarer
♠ A 9 7 5 4

Dummy
♠ Q 10 3 2

Most banged down the ace and then led low. Too bad, the K-J-6 were sitting over the dummy.

Sammy Kehela, playing with Eric Murray, had some good and bad news to tell about this one. The good news was that he led the queen of spades from the dummy to hold his spade losers to one. The bad news was that he was in seven spades. The final bit of news was that he got an average.

I must say that of all the boards I played in New Orleans, the round against the Australians, Ron Klinger and Don Evans, stands out.

This was the first board, with Evans North, and Klinger South.

North dealer
Both sides vulnerable

North
♠ A K J 2
♡ 9 6 4
♢ A 8 7
♣ Q 6 4

West
♠ 10 8 4
♡ 3
♢ J 10 9 5 3
♣ A 8 7 3

East
♠ 5
♡ J 10 7 5 2
♢ Q 6 4 2
♣ J 9 2

South
♠ Q 9 7 6 3
♡ A K Q 8
♢ K
♣ K 10 5

This was the bidding with East-West silent:

Evans	Klinger
North	South
1 ♣	1 ♠
1 NT	2 NT
4 ♠	4 NT
5 ♡	5 ♠
6 ♣	6 ♠

The two notrump bid was alerted, but we elected to wait until the end of the auction for the explanations. Klinger began to explain when Evans interrupted him. "Let me tell you what this all means," he said.

"Two notrump is forcing and asks for more definition. My four spade bid showed "brilliant spades" (I loved that) and four notrump was Blackwood. Five hearts showed two aces and five spades was to play. My six club bid showed the *king* and six spades was to play. I've goofed terribly and I apologize.

Well, I thought, sitting East after the dummy came down, they must be off two aces (why isn't Billy leading one?), and certainly there has been a big misunderstanding here. Maybe they have been reading about some of our lulus and have decided to throw us a bone.

The next thing I know Klinger is winning the heart lead (don't tell me my guy is underleading one of his aces), playing a spade and claiming! Claiming after all that! It's like giving candy to a baby and then taking it away just as he is about to eat it.

The second board was even more exciting after Klinger missorted his hand to produce this series of events:

West dealer
Neither side vulnerable
(Positions rearranged for convenience.)

```
                          North
                          ♠ 9
                          ♡ K Q 9 6 4
                          ◇ Q 6 3
                          ♣ A 4 3 2
        West                              East
        ♠ 5 4 3                           ♠ K J 10 7
        ♡ J 10 7 2                        ♡ A 8 5
        ◇ 4                               ◇ K 10 8
        ♣ K Q J 10 7                      ♣ 9 8 5
                          South
                          ♠ A Q 8 6 2
                          ♡ 3
                          ◇ A J 9 7 5 2
                          ♣ 6
```

Me	*Klinger*	*Billy*	*Evans*
West	North	East	South
pass	1 ♣ !	1 ♠	2 ◇
2 ♠	3 ◇	pass	4 NT
pass	5 ◇	pass	6 ◇
(all pass)			

Opening lead: ♣ K

When Evans got a load of the dummy, all he could say was
"well stroke me naked." But he almost made it. If diamonds had
been 2-2 he would have. He hooked the queen of spades and led
a heart to the king and ace. The club return was ruffed, a spade
ruffed low in dummy, a spade pitched on a high heart and a club
ruffed back to the closed hand. A second spade was ruffed in
dummy, but Billy had to make a trump trick for down one. So
much for the Australians.

Billy was in top form himself. On one hand he held:

♠ A 9 ♡ 7 6 ◇ A 9 6 4 ♣ A K 7 5 2.

The vulnerable opponent to his left opened three spades, and when this came around to him he tried three notrump. The only problem was that I had overcalled four hearts in between! No problem, he raised to six hearts and I held:

♠ — ♡ A Q 8 5 3 2 ◇ K Q 10 2 ♣ 10 4 3.

The king of hearts was onside and it was our best bid slam.

On another hand we had a giant misunderstanding over a four notrump takeout bid, and Billy wound up playing five hearts doubled, vulnerable, with K-x-x-x opposite x-x as his trump suit—with a few other losers as well.

As this was the last board of the round and there were time penalties, it was becoming obvious (after we were already down five) that this was not going to be one of our better results. Late in the hand a heart was led through Billy's king and he went into the tank.

I told him not to worry about it; after all, what did it matter if we went down six or seven; besides we were behind. "Just a minute," says Billy, "I want to figure this out." Shades of Marshall Miles.

Jerusalem, 1983. Left to right: Christian Mari, Yvonne, me, Billy, Paul Chemla, and Armand Cohen.

Later Billy produced what must have been one of the best plays of the tournament.

South dealer
Both sides vulnerable

North
♠ A 2
♡ Q 9 8 7 3
◊ J 10 5 4
♣ K 4

West (Billy)
♠ K J 6 5
♡ A J 6
◊ 9 7 6
♣ 10 9 3

East
♠ 10 8 7
♡ 10 5 2
◊ K 3 2
♣ Q J 6 5

South
♠ Q 9 4 3
♡ K 4
◊ A Q 8
♣ A 8 7 2

After a Precision one notrump opening, South became declarer in three notrump, and Billy got off to the best lead of the ten of clubs. Declarer won the king and led a diamond to the queen, followed by a low heart. Billy played the *jack*. Declarer won in dummy and ran the jack of diamonds, followed by a diamond to his ace. He now exited with the king of hearts to Billy's ace. Billy played the nine of clubs and a club to declarer's ace, leaving:

```
                        North
                        ♠ A 2
                        ♡ 9 8
                        ◊ 10
                        ♣ —
West                                      East
♠ K J 6 5                                 ♠ 10 8 7
♡ 6                                       ♡ 10
◊ —                                       ◊ —
♣ —                                       ♣ Q
                        South
                        ♠ Q 9 4 3
                        ♡ —
                        ◊ —
                        ♣ 8
```

Declarer led a spade to dummy and cashed the good diamond. If Billy had not made the earlier heart play, he would now have had a choice of endplays: he could keep his high heart and be thrown in with a heart to lead from his king of spades; or he could jettison his high heart on the thirteenth diamond, and lead from his spade king when declarer played a spade off the board and put in the nine. As it was, there was no problem defeating three notrump.

However, the very best play of the tournament was when one of the French women decided to go topless at the pool. Of course, this is an ordinary occurrence in France, but in New Orleans it was something else.

First, there was a huge office building overlooking the pool and word spread like wildfire. Almost every window had four or five noses pressed against it. Some of the more sophisticated started to bring binoculars when they realized that this was going to be a regular thing.

As all good things must come to an end, so it came to pass that the police showed up one morning and told the young lady that she was disrupting work in the big building and someone had complained. The Solomonic decision was to let her go topless on the weekends when the office building was closed, but cover up during working days.

I would like to finish up with a description of the Swiss Teams. Let me say that nobody has ever played in a Swiss Teams like this before.

The Knockouts started like this. Each team played a sixteen board match. If you won that match you were free for the rest of the day, and eligible to play the next day in the Knockouts with the other winners. If you lost that match you played another sixteen board match against one of the other losers. If you won that match you went right back into the Knockouts. If you lost that match you were sent to a version of hell that only those who lost those first two matches can really understand.

Those who lost their first two matches had to play in an "Endless Swiss" from which one, and only one, team would emerge to get back into the Knockouts.

The problem was that each session the teams who lost in the Knockouts would join the Swiss Teams with a predetermined score—which was approximately the same as that of the team who was leading the Swiss.

So no matter how well you were doing, you knew that, in a few hours, a whole new wave of players would be coming at you with a big score, bigger than yours—unless you happened to be leading by a wide margin.

Bob Hamman, who didn't have to go through this, likened it to a marathon race where your opponent drops out every so often and has a fresh replacement waiting, while you continue running with your tongue hanging out.

Perhaps you can figure out from this whether our team was in the Swiss Teams or not. Very good.

Our team won 17 of 20 matches and finished nowhere, because we lost two of our last three matches. (Matches at the end had a total of 60 victory points available; earlier in the week 20, and then 40, victory points were available.)

Finally, because our team was leading in the Swiss for a long time, we had to play the second place team each time. And if after that match the same two teams were still in first and second place we had to play them again . . . and again.

As a result, we played the same team (Sontag-Weichsel, Silverman-Lipsitz, Andersen-McLean) *six* times.

Here is an Eric Murray bidding problem from the Endless Swiss. With both sides vulnerable, playing with a very conservative partner, you look at this hand in fourth seat with three passes to you: ♠ 6 5 3 ♡ J 7 6 5 ◇ 10 7 6 4 3 ♣ 7.

You play four-card majors and Drury. What do you do?

Murray, having noticed small beads of sweat trickle down his partner's forehead, studied his cards. After much soul-searching he passed . . . and then grabbed everyone's hand before they could put it back in the board.

Only Sammy Kehela, his partner, refused to let go of his cards. He had played his "PASS" card by mistake, holding:

♠ J 10 9 ♡ A Q 8 ◇ A ♣ A K J 5 4 3.

As usual, all's well that ends well. The other team got too high with these cards, and the upshot is that Eric has a great deal more respect for Kehela's passes.

Alan Sontag, once my frequent opponent, now my frequent partner, relaxes behind screens while waiting for me to bid.

Presenting a check to charity with Jane Fonda, Mary Jane Farrell, and Freddie Sheinwold at the Wild Whist Bridge Club in California.

Yes, Billy!

LAST APRIL Billy Eisenberg, David Berkowitz, John Solodar and I were invited to Leeds, England, to participate in the Continental Life Insurance Co. knockout team championship.

In the final I picked up the following hand, not vul vs. vul, as North: ♠ J 6 5 ♡ J ◊ A Q 9 3 2 ♣ A Q 8 7.

	Me		*Billy*
West	North	East	South
—	—	—	1 ♣
3 ♡	?		

Not knowing what to do, I decided to apply a slight addition to "Hamman's Law," * which clearly states: if a number of bids are possible and three notrump is one of them, bid it." The adjunct states: if a number of bids are possible and one of them does not get you past three notrump, for God's sake bid it! I therefore made a negative double, intending to pull a three spades response to five clubs. The bidding continued:

---

* See page 74 for the complete list of Hamman's rules. I refuse to repeat them all a *third* time!

	Me		*Billy*
West	North	East	South
—	—	—	1 ♣
3 ♡	double	4 ♡	pass
pass	?		

(My hand: ♠ J 6 5 ♡ J ◇ A Q 9 3 2 ♣ A Q 8 7.)

Never having discussed the meaning of four notrump in this sequence, I opted for a quiet five clubs which ended the bidding . . . but not the postmortem. Billy held:

♠ A K 3 ♡ 6 2 ◇ K 5 ♣ K 10 6 5 3 2.

The thought crossed my mind that Billy had a pretty good hand on the bidding. We had missed a cold slam (another one) and I braced myself for the inevitable.

"Why didn't you bid a simple four hearts over three hearts? It's a baby bid. If you do, we roll into six clubs."

"I was afraid we'd miss three notrump. What if you had a minimum balanced hand with some heart strength?"

"Now listen to me, and don't ever forget this. Whenever they preempt, vulnerable, you can forget about my having opened a three-card suit. Furthermore, it is unlikely that I will have two heart stoppers. Besides, all you had to do was bid four notrump over four hearts and I would have leaped to six clubs."

"Yes, Billy."

We now change the scene. It is nine months later and I am on the phone with Billy bidding bridge hands. I had just received twelve back issues of the British publication "Bridge." There were bidding problem inserts in each magazine. I gave Billy the West hands and I kept the East hands. He even xeroxed his so he could keep one copy at home.

We try to bid one set each day but it is difficult. Billy has much to say after nearly every hand, and besides, he is at work. From time to time he cuts me off when he gets a call (usually from another bridge player) which interrupts the natural flow of our beautiful bidding.

Imagine my surprise when I noticed that the hand we had misbid to five clubs *was one of the problems.* I had my old hand and Billy had his. I recognized the hand, Billy did not.

The instructions read there would be an interference overcall of three hearts. Our new bidding sequence started:

Billy		*Me*	
West	North	East	South
1 ♣	3 ♡	?	

This time I did not hesitate; a lesson given is a lesson learned. I bid a confident four hearts, agreeing clubs, confirming a heart control, and showing slam interest—all of the things Billy told me my bid would have shown.

Billy cue-bid four spades. I bid five clubs. Billy passed! There we were in five clubs again. Just let him say anything this time.

It turned out that Billy wanted to bid Blackwood, but he was afraid I might have only one ace, and he couldn't handle a five diamond response.

After nine months I was ready for that one. He had forgotten our system! We play that when clubs is the agreed suit and the player being asked about aces has shown a strong hand, we eliminate the zero response and start with one. Therefore, a five club response would have shown one (or four) key cards. He had nothing to fear.

"I'm sorry," said Billy, "I blew it."

"Yes, Billy."

Do you play inverted minors, by the way? I don't but I have been thinking about switching. This was the hand that made me reconsider. First the prologue.

We were playing in the Maccabiah Games in Israel against Israel, and Billy was the official scorekeeper for the table (a serious error). After we had completed the first hand, Billy entered the score and was about to remove the next hand from the board when an old friend came up to the table and chatted with Billy—making dinner plans. Fine. Now on to the next hand.

Billy was looking at:

♠ K ♡ A K J 2 ◇ A K Q J 10 9 ♣ Q 4.

He decided to open two clubs. So he carefully put his "2 ♣" card on the table. (The entire tournament was played with bidding boxes.)

Then Billy decided to look up and see what was going on. What he saw was that I had opened the bidding one club, the next hand had passed, and Billy had given me a very comfortable raise to two clubs with his 23-count!

To say that he tried to grab his card off the table is the understatement of the year. Knowing that four drinks and two kibitzers toppled over after his majestic sweep might give you the picture. In any case, the director was summoned and didn't buy Billy's story that the "2 ♣" card never actually hit the table! The two club bid had to stand. We were vulnerable! Next hand passed and the bidding came back to me. Now do you understand why I wish I was playing inverted minors? The two club raise would have been forcing.

No matter. It seemed that I had two choices. Report back to my team that we had played either a vulnerable slam or a grand slam in two clubs, or bid again and spend the rest of my life in an Israeli prison.

Fortunately, my hand was:

♠ A Q 4 ♡ 7 3 ◇ 3 2 ♣ A K J 9 7 3.

I felt I could ethically bid three clubs without any of those guys hanging around the table with the machine guns coming over. The three club bid was greeted by Billy whipping out his "4 NT" card. After that we steamed into seven notrump. No problem, just another routine grand . . . with Billy.

IV
Still More Partners

A Record, I Think

I TEACH MY BEGINNERS that if both hands are balanced they should be in three notrump if they have 25-32 points. I tell them that even though most books say that they need 26, after I am through teaching them how to play the hand, they will be able to make three notrump with at least one point less.

Getting back to the real world, we have all seen hands come home with 22 or so points if there is a long suit, or if one opponent has too many high cards and must make some critical discards.

On the other side of the ledger there are those 4-3-3-3 hands that face each other with the defenders mockingly resisting every effort that the declarer makes to bring in nine tricks with a combined count of 27-28 high card points.

My own personal record, and one I have not bragged about too often, is going down in three notrump with 29 points between the two hands and no unstopped suit. It wasn't easy, you understand, but after a couple of finesses lost, and a couple of other suits didn't break, and I misread the end position, I managed to wind up with only eight. This happened 17 years ago, and until the following deal I felt secure that 29 would be my limit.

Playing in a friendly rubber game not long ago, I dealt myself and the table this layout:

South dealer
Both sides vulnerable

```
                        North
                        ♠ Q J 6
                        ♡ A K 5
                        ◇ J 7 4
                        ♣ J 9 5 4
        West                            East
        ♠ 10 9 8 7 4 3                  ♠ 2
        ♡ Q 10 8 6                      ♡ 9 7 3
        ◇ 9 3 2                         ◇ K Q 6 5
        ♣ —                            ♣ Q 10 8 6 3
                        South
                        ♠ A K 5
                        ♡ J 4 2
                        ◇ A 10 8
                        ♣ A K 7 2
```

Me

South	West	North	East
1 ♣	pass	1 ◇	pass
2 NT	pass	3 NT	(all pass)

Opening lead: ♠ 10

My partner, who had witnessed some of my previous notrump adventures over the years, cautiously raised me to game with his balanced 12.

Quickly and confidently, I won the spade in my hand and led the king of clubs. When West discarded a spade, the play slowed down to such an extent that my partner finally asked me if I was all right.

In fact, I was in a mild state of shock. Knowing that I now had only eight sure tricks, instead of being able to think about the best way to secure nine, all I could think was: "Kantar, you have 31 points between these two hands. For God's sake, figure something out or you will never live this one down."

Ever so daintily I crossed to the heart king and led a low diamond. East played the six. Still on top of my game, I stuck in the eight, knowing, just knowing, that the nine would appear.

It did.

West got out with a spade and East discarded a heart (he should have thrown a club) and I won on the table.

Could this really be happening to a great player like me? At least, I had formulated a plan. (I was going to have to tell my partner something after this hand was over.) If I could somehow strip East of his red cards I could duck a club and force East to lead away from his queen of clubs; and this hand would just go down as another tough struggle, but not too tough. (Fifteen minutes had already elapsed.)

I now led a second diamond from the table and ducked East's queen. East returned a heart, and once again I realized I had a problem. This was the actual end position, just one card removed from what I thought it was:

```
                    North
                    ♠ Q
                    ♡ A 5
                    ◊ J
                    ♣ J 9 5
West                                East
♠ 9 8 7                             ♠ —
♡ Q 10 8                            ♡ 9
◊ 2                                 ◊ K 5
♣ —                                 ♣ Q 10 8 6
                    South
                    ♠ A
                    ♡ J 4
                    ◊ A
                    ♣ A 7 2
```

With the actual position I can win the ace of hearts, cash my diamond and spade winners, and toss East in with a low club. East cashes a diamond, upon which I throw losing hearts from both hands, but is finally forced to lead away from that queen of clubs for my ninth trick.

However, I thought that East had one more heart and one less diamond. If that is the case I cannot win the ace of hearts and cash a spade because East will then have a heart to get to West's spades.

```
                    North
                    ♠ Q
                    ♡ A 5
                    ◊ J
                    ♣ J 9 5
      West                          East
      ♠ 9 8 7                       ♠ —
      ♡ Q 10 8                      ♡ 9
      ◊ 2                           ◊ K 5
      ♣ —                           ♣ Q 10 8 6
                    South
                    ♠ A
                    ♡ J 4
                    ◊ A
                    ♣ A 7 2
```

If my idea was right, I could make the hand thus: duck the heart, win any return, cash my spade, heart and diamond winners, and duck a club. Furthermore, if I was wrong and the cards were as they actually were, West would have to win the heart return and play specifically a diamond—or else I would still make the hand on a funny squeeze.

To make a long story a bit sadder, I ducked the heart and West shifted to a diamond. Now there was no way. I was finished. Down one with 31 points between the two hands. Did I have a new record? I would have to wait until Guiness' next book came out. In the meantime I am advising my classes that they must have at least 27 high card points between the two hands to have a fairly good chance at three notrump.

NIGHTMARE
Seven Blunders, All in a Row

HOW CAN I word this? Let's try this: What is the greatest number of consecutive hands you have played in which you committed one sort of a blunder or another?

My current record is seven, and I found a very convenient time to pull off this coup—the recent Vanderbilt Cup Matches at the National Championships in Detroit.

Our team was playing a third round match and we were 19 IMPs down at half-time.

Playing with Mike Lawrence in the third quarter, the first few boards were uneventful. But then came the "streak."

It isn't that I relish going over this "streak" in print, but I do have my reasons. They are:

(1) I will purge myself once and for all.

(2) It will give you a chance to see if you could have done better (I am making this into a quiz). Believe me, you will do better.

(3) I was told to write an instructive article. In a way, this will be an instructive article—what not to bid, what not to play, and what not to lead.

Hand #1 is a bidding problem. Both sides are vulnerable, and you, South, hold: ♠ Q 4 ♡ J 7 6 4 ◊ A Q 10 9 8 ♣ J 8.

The opponents are playing Precision. The bidding proceeds:

West	North	East	South (you)
1 ♠	pass	1 NT˙	pass
2 ♣˙˙	pass	pass	?

˙ Forcing
˙˙ Could be a three card suit

Hand #2 is an opening lead problem.
This time you hold: ♠ 4 ♡ J 10 7 6 3 2 ◊ 10 9 5 ♣ 10 7 3.

South	West (you)	North	East
1 ♠	pass	3 ♠˙	pass
4 ♠	(all pass)		

˙ Limit Raise

What do you lead?

Hand #3 is a bidding and a play problem. First decide what you would bid before going on to the play.

You hold: ♠ 10 4 3 2 ♡ 7 6 2 ◊ A 10 9 6 ♣ K 4.

West	North	East	South (you)
—	1 ♣	pass	1 ◊
pass	1 ♡	pass	?

Assume you rebid one notrump. Of course, it works out much better to rebid one spade, but you are on your "streak." In any case, your rebid ends the auction.

North
♠ K Q 7 5
♡ K Q 9 4
◇ 4
♣ Q J 6 5

South
♠ 10 4 3 2
♡ 7 6 2
◇ A 10 9 6
♣ K 4

West, Dave Berkowitz, leads the heart ten (showing 0 or 2 higher cards) and East, Harold Lilie, plays low under the queen.

Right or wrong, you lead the spade king off dummy and West, Berkowitz, wins and returns the eight of hearts. Plan the play.

Hand #4 is a defensive problem. To make things easier, you will be sitting West. You hold: ♠ K 10 8 5 ♡ Q J 6 3 ◇ J 5 ♣ J 6 3.

West (you)	North	East	South
—	1 ◇	pass	1 ♡
pass	1 ♠	pass	1 NT
(all pass)			

Decide upon your opening lead.

North (dummy)
♠ A J 7 2
♡ 7 4 2
◇ A Q 10 7
♣ Q 9

West (you)
♠ K 10 8 5
♡ Q J 6 3
◇ J 5
♣ J 6 3

I elected to lead the three of hearts. Partner won the ace and returned the ten, declarer playing low. Plan your defense.

Hand #5 is a bidding problem. Both sides are vulnerable and you hold: ♠ 10 9 2 ♡ K 7 6 5 4 3 ◇ K J 4 2 ♣ —.

West	North	East	South (you)
—	—	1 ♠	pass
1 NT*	pass	2 ♣	pass
2 ♠	pass	pass	?

* Forcing

(1) Would you have passed over two clubs?

(2) What do you do now, having passed both times previous?

Hands #6 and #7 are particularly painful because stupidity is now entering into the picture. Until now I had one reason or another for my errors. But these last two . . .

Hand #6
North dealer
Both sides vulnerable

North
♠ A Q J 5
♡ K 10 7 3
◇ A Q 9
♣ K 6

South
♠ 10 8 7 6
♡ A 8 4 2
◇ 7 5 4
♣ J 7

West	North	East	South (you)
—	1 ◇	pass	1 ♡
pass	4 ♡	(all pass)	

Opening lead: ♠ 2

(Answer each question before going on to the next.)

(1) Which spade do you play from dummy?

(2) Assume you play the queen and it wins. What is your next play(s)?

(3) Assume you play the king and seven of hearts to the ace, West playing the queen on the second round. What do you do now?

(4) Assume you lead the ten of spades which is covered and ruffed by East with the heart jack. East now exits with a diamond to the ten and queen. Now what?

Hand #7
This one really hurts. With both sides vulnerable you pick up:
♠ 10 8 ♡ A K 4 ◇ J 9 3 ♣ A Q 10 3 2. The bidding proceeds:

South	West (you)	North	East
1 ◇ˑ	pass	1 ♠	pass
2 ♣	?		

ˑCould be a short suit. If it is, clubs is the long suit.

Right or wrong (you will see soon enough) I passed. The final contract became two clubs and I led the king of hearts.

North (dummy)
♠ K Q 9 3 2
♡ 9 8 2
◇ Q 10
♣ 9 5 4

West (you)
♠ 10 8
♡ A K 4
◇ J 9 3
♣ A Q 10 3 2

Partner plays the seven of hearts and declarer the three. What do you play next?

Part II - What I Should Have Done

Hand #1

                    North
                    ♠ K J 10 7 2
                    ♡ 10 5 3
                    ◊ K
                    ♣ K 10 4 2

West   East
♠ A 9 8 5 3   ♠ 6
♡ K 9 2   ♡ A Q 8
◊ 7 6   ◊ J 5 4 3 2
♣ A 9 5   ♣ Q 7 6 3

                    South
                    ♠ Q 4
                    ♡ J 7 6 4
                    ◊ A Q 10 9 8
                    ♣ J 8

I bid two diamonds. This got doubled by East. In the play I went down an extra trick, losing 800 points on the deal. Had I doubled two clubs, and had my partner passed, we would have beaten the contract one trick with good defense. At the other table they passed the hand out!

Hand #2

North
♠ K Q 10 3 2
♡ K 9 4
◊ Q 7 6
♣ 6 5

West
♠ 4
♡ J 10 7 6 3 2
◊ 10 9 5
♣ 10 7 3

East
♠ 8 5
♡ A Q
◊ A 8 4 3 2
♣ K Q J 8

South
♠ A J 9 7 6
♡ 8 5
◊ K J
♣ A 9 4 2

I led the ten of diamonds and the hand can no longer be defeated. Declarer was able to discard a losing heart on a diamond.

Only a heart lead defeats the game. (If a club is led, declarer simply ducks the first trick, thus depriving West of a later club entry for a heart play.) At the other table the lead was the jack of hearts—naturally.

Hand #3

                        North
                        ♠ K Q 7 5
                        ♡ K Q 9 4
                        ◊ 4
                        ♣ Q J 6 5
        West   East
        ♠ A J 9   ♠ 8 6
        ♡ A 10 8   ♡ J 5 3
        ◊ K 8 3   ◊ Q J 7 5 2
        ♣ A 9 8 3   ♣ 10 7 2
                        South
                        ♠ 10 4 3 2
                        ♡ 7 6 2
                        ◊ A 10 9 6
                        ♣ K 4

I stuck in the nine which lost to the jack. Back came a low diamond. My ten lost to the king and I won the diamond continuation.

I played a third heart to the ace. West continued with a diamond to the queen. East now played his remaining spade. There was no way I could avoid going down one trick. (What an opening lead!)

At the other table they played in a spade partial and made four.

Hand #4

```
                        North
                        ♠ A J 7 2
                        ♡ 7 4 2
                        ◊ A Q 10 7
                        ♣ Q 9
West                                        East
♠ K 10 8 5                                  ♠ 6 4
♡ Q J 6 3                                   ♡ A 10
◊ J 5                                       ◊ K 9 4 3
♣ J 6 3                                     ♣ K 10 8 7 5
                        South
                        ♠ Q 9 3
                        ♡ K 9 8 5
                        ◊ 8 6 2
                        ♣ A 4 2
```

I overtook the ten of hearts to make the "killing" shift—the ten of spades. In the books and the newspaper columns, declarer has 9-x or x-x in spades and you get your name in print for making this great play. Suffice to say that it was not the killing shift.

As I recall, declarer played the jack (?) from dummy and then a low spade to the queen and king. Working out the position perfectly, I shifted to a low diamond! Michael is still waiting for a club play.

The upshot was that an overtrick was scored. At the other table one notrump was defeated. "How?" I asked. "Clubs were led." "Oh."

Hand #5

                              North
                              ♠ 8 7
                              ♡ A Q 2
                              ◊ 9 6 5
                              ♣ A Q J 7 2
        West   East
        ♠ A 6 5   ♠ K Q J 4 3
        ♡ J 9   ♡ 10 8
        ◊ 8 7 3   ◊ A Q 10
        ♣ 10 9 8 4 3   ♣ K 6 5
                              South
                              ♠ 10 9 2
                              ♡ K 7 6 5 4 3
                              ◊ K J 4 2
                              ♣ —

With paranoia setting in, I visualized a doubleton spade to my
left with many clubs in partner's hand. Fearing hearts to my left, I
meekly passed.

Notice with the favorable diamond position we have a game.
We beat two spades one trick. A plus score! Push board. Same
result at the other table.

Hand #6

```
                        North
                        ♠ A Q J 5
                        ♡ K 10 7 3
                        ◊ A Q 9
                        ♣ K 6
        West                                East
        ♠ K 9 3 2                           ♠ 4
        ♡ Q 9                               ♡ J 6 5
        ◊ K J 10 6                          ◊ 8 3 2
        ♣ Q 10 8                            ♣ A 9 5 4 3 2
                        South
                        ♠ 10 8 7 6
                        ♡ A 8 4 2
                        ◊ 7 5 4
                        ♣ J 7
```

This happens to be a very interesting play and defense problem. The way the play actually came up, my play was clear.

I should cross to my hand with a trump, eliminate the spades, and play ace and a diamond. West wins and exits with a low club. Now I must guess the club position.

Why I didn't do this, I still don't know. Had East *not* ruffed the spade (best), the hand can still be made on a strange squeeze.

I exit with a trump and East wins and returns a diamond. On the trump exit, West discards a club. Now I cross to my hand with a trump (the hand is now being played in notrump), and West must find a second discard. If he discards a club, blanking the queen, I have no trouble if I read the position.

Assume West discards a diamond. I cash two more spades and exit with ace and a diamond. Again West leads a club and again I must guess the position.

The hand is easier to play if the opening lead is ducked and a second spade played immediately.

At the other table North played a cozy one trump, just making with a club lead.

Hand #7 (You don't really want to see this one, do you? Or are you loving every minute of this?)

North
♠ K Q 9 3 2
♡ 9 8 2
◇ Q 10
♣ 9 5 4

West
♠ 10 8
♡ A K 4
◇ J 9 3
♣ A Q 10 3 2

East
♠ A J 7 6 5 4
♡ Q 7 5
◇ 7 6 4
♣ 6

South
♠ —
♡ J 10 6 3
◇ A K 8 5 2
♣ K J 8 7

At trick two I shifted to the ten of spades. (I was afraid partner had the J-10-7 of hearts.) Declarer ruffed out the ace, and played four rounds of diamonds discarding the remaining hearts from dummy. Had I discarded my spade on the fourth diamond I would have defeated the hand easily. But no, I ruffed.

Incredibly, I exited with a heart! (Dear God, why am I telling everybody this?) Declarer ruffed, ruffed a spade back to his hand, ruffed yet another heart, and then exited with a high spade, which I ruffed. Down to a trump flush I had to concede the eighth trick to the king of clubs.

At the other table, with less "imaginative" defense, two clubs was defeated by two tricks. By the way, did you double? If you did, you collected 500 points. To make a sad story sadder, our team lost 43 IMPs in this quarter—the exact amount that we lost on the boards that you have just seen.

Yes, our team lost the match. Yes, I did not play the fourth quarter. What have I learned from all this? Three things: (1) During a nightmare, do not dwell on previous bad results. Things only get worse. History is history. (2) Play better. (3) If this should ever happen again, don't write about it!

Misery at the Bridge Table

FIRST, A COUPLE of hands from the Life Master Pairs in Boston. Peter Weichsel, playing with Neil Silverman, arrived in six diamonds after a tortuous sequence that left the pair in time trouble.

```
                    North
                    ♠ A K 9
                    ♡ A K Q 9 8 7
                    ◇ A Q 2
                    ♣ 2
West                                    East
♠ Q 10 3                                ♠ 8 6 2
♡ 6 5                                   ♡ J 10 4 3 2
◇ 8 4 3                                 ◇ 9 7 6
♣ A 10 9 8 7                            ♣ 4 3
                    South (Peter)
                    ♠ J 7 5 4
                    ♡ —
                    ◇ K J 10 5
                    ♣ K Q J 6 5
```

West led the three of spades and Peter went into a long huddle, deciding how to play this awkward hand. He considered letting the opening lead ride around to his jack, but finally went up ace, East playing the *deuce*.

At trick two he led a club to the king and ace, and when West returned the ten of spades, Peter put his head in his hands and tried to work out what was going on in the spade suit. In the meantime, directors were hovering around the table attempting to speed up the action.

North
♠ A K 9
♡ A K Q 9 8 7
◊ A Q 2
♣ 2

West
♠ Q 10 3
♡ 6 5
◊ 8 4 3
♣ A 10 9 8 7

East
♠ 8 6 2
♡ J 10 4 3 2
◊ 9 7 6
♣ 4 3

South (Peter)
♠ J 7 5 4
♡ —
◊ K J 10 5
♣ K Q J 6 5

Again Peter had to decide whether to let that spade come around or hope for good breaks in both red suits. The spade return had destroyed any black suit squeeze he may have had against West.

After lengthy reflection Peter decided the hell with it; he was going to let the spade run to his jack. After all, hadn't East played the deuce of spades at trick one? Would he have played that way with Q-x-x? Hardly.

Just as Peter was about to call small from the dummy, East blurted out, "I forgot to tell you, we play upside down attitude signals!"

This meant, of course, that East's deuce at trick one was actually a come-on signal in spades. Armed with new information, Peter went up with the ace of spades and went down two tricks.

Going down two on this hand was not a good result. In fact, out of a possible 29 matchpoints, Peter and Neil got only two. Peter decided to ask for a committee meeting; East's comment had been intentionally misleading.

No matter. The committee allowed the result to stand, and the directors fined Peter an additional four points for slow play. So he and Neil wound up with minus two matchpoints on the board.

If you think that is a sad story, I have a sadder one. I'm sure most of you have heard about this hand, also from the Life Master's Pairs in Boston; but just in case:

North (me)
♠ K Q J 5 3
♡ 10 5
◇ 7 5 4
♣ 8 4 2

West
♠ 10 8 7
♡ J
◇ Q J 10 9 8
♣ Q 9 6 5

East
♠ 9 6 4 2
♡ 8 4 2
◇ 6 2
♣ K J 7 3

South (Michael)
♠ A
♡ A K Q 9 7 6 3
◇ A K 3
♣ A 10

My partner, Mike Lawrence, and I arrived in seven notrump played by Michael after I had rebid spades and preferred hearts. Michael was hoping I had the jack of hearts or the queen of diamonds for an entry to the spades. This was matchpoints where it pays to take an occasional risk for a top score.

In any case, the queen of diamonds was led. There was no jack of hearts, no queen of diamonds, and no dummy entry to the spades. The next problem was how to play this hand at Matchpoints. At rubber bridge there is no alternative. Win the opening lead, cash the ace of spades and play a high heart, hoping the jack falls singleton. If it does, congratulate yourselves on great bidding. If not, try to figure out where your partner went wrong in the auction.

If you cash a high heart and the jack of hearts is not singleton, you must go down two tricks. On the other hand, if you cash the ace of spades and lead the nine of hearts, somebody will probably win the jack (this is seven notrump after all), providing an entry to get rid of both minor suit losers. Down only one.

The problem was to try to guess where the field would be. Obviously if no one was in slam it would be crazy to play for a minus score when everyone else would be plus. On the other hand, if other pairs reached seven, or even six notrump, it would probably be worthwhile to go down only one.

In any case, Michael decided to play for down one. He cashed the ace of spades and led the nine of hearts. We both saw the jack of hearts leap out of the West hand. It was singleton after all!

Once Michael assured himself that he had lost to a singleton jack he began to systematically rip up his cards! Then he realized we still had another round to play. It is rumored that the next player, picking up the shredded cards, passed the hand out. He knew something terrible was about to happen and wasn't in the mood to find out what. P.S. If Michael lays down the heart ace at trick three we win the event.

More Mike Lawrence. We were defending one notrump and this was the layout of the spade suit:

```
                    North (dummy)
                    ♠ 10 9 7 6
West (me)                              East (Michael)
♠ K 3 2                                ♠ Q 8 4
                    South
                    ♠ A J 5
```

Declarer had denied four spades during the bidding and I decided to lead the deuce of spades. Dummy played low and Michael quite properly played the eight, catering to declarer holding either K-J, A-J, K-x or A-x.

The eight lost to the jack and declarer took a losing finesse in another suit into my hand. I thought that declarer might have started with the spade A-J blank and smartly continued with the three of spades.

Declarer played the ten from dummy and Michael, thinking that I had four spades, also thought that declarer held the A-J doubleton. As a result, he played low a second time expecting the ace to come down.

It did come down all right, and when it did it brought down my queen and Michael's king with a thundering crash.

There's more. Playing with Michael in a National Open Pairs, I picked up the following hand with neither side vulnerable:

♠ K 10 4 3 ♡ Q 8 7 ◇ Q J 8 ♣ A 7 6.

We had an agreement not to open twelve-point dogs, but I fell from grace and opened one club. Next hand overcalled four hearts, and Michael was looking at:

♠ Q J 9 7 6 2 ♡ A ◇ A K ♣ Q 10 5 4.

Fearing we could have a slam, and that I would be likely to pass a four spade response, Michael leaped to six clubs, which became the final contract.

The opponents led a heart and I studied the dummy thoughtfully. Actually, I was wondering what I was going to say after the debacle was over. Recklessly, I glanced at Michael who was mouthing, "Do we have a play?"

I couldn't resist. "Yes, Michael," I said, "if the K-J-9 sixth of clubs is singleton I am cold for the hand."

Playing with Michael in a Regional Open Pairs in Houston, we found ourselves ringed with kibitzers. If they were looking for excitement they didn't have to wait long.

Along about the fourth round Michael opened one spade, next hand passed and I was looking at:

♠ — ♡ A K 9 8 6 5 4 ◇ A 7 6 5 ♣ Q J.

After some thought I decided to try a jump shift to three hearts to see what would happen. "Alert" says Michael. What is it, they ask.

"It shows an unknown singleton with at least four-card spade support. Four spades," says Michael.

Now it all came back to me. I had agreed to this convention some time ago and had completely forgotten. Apparently, I was faced with an ethical problem which didn't even enter my mind at the time. I wanted to play in hearts!

I tried five hearts. "Alert" says Michael. What is it, they ask. "He has a heart void." With this holding:

♠ A K Q 10 8 ♡ J 3 2 ◇ K J ♣ 10 7 6,

Michael leaped to six spades. Well, there was no stopping me now. I bid seven hearts. "Alert," screams Michael. What is it, they ask. "Cancel all previous alerts, I pass."

Well, they led a diamond and I made seven hearts. (East had the ace-king of clubs.) But wait, where did all the kibitzers go?

When I first started playing with Michael I mailed him a zillion pages of methods and conventions that I hoped we could play together. Now that I am a bit older and wiser I realize that the worst thing you can do to a new partner is to make him play the way you want to play.

Several weeks after I sent Michael the slew of conventions, I met him at a tournament and asked him if he knew all of "our" conventions.

He answered, "Not exactly. I plan to bid three notrump as fast as I can and hope it is not a convention."

I have saved my favorite Lawrence story for the end. One day he was playing rubber bridge with Harold Guiver and they embarked upon a very scientific auction where every suit except clubs had been bid and supported. Finally, the bid came back to Lawrence and he decided to make the master bid of seven clubs, the unbid suit (he happened to have the stiff ace), asking Harold to pick the best grand slam.

Harold, holding Q-x-x of clubs, thought that Lawrence had been sitting in the bushes for the entire auction and actually had clubs. Furthermore, he thought that his queen of clubs was the key card to insure the grand. He passed!

The opening lead was made and Harold put down two small clubs, saving his queen as a big surprise. Finally, when he triumphantly revealed the club queen, Michael said, "Oh, you clever little devil, you." Down six.

Michael chuckles as he sits down to play.

Michael waits for Harold to bid over seven clubs.

"Oh, you clever little devil, you."

Key Cards

PLAYING WITH P.O. (Per Olov) Sundelin, the Swedish star, in the Blue Ribbon Pairs, our "experienced" partnership had the following to contend with:

West (me)	East (P.O.)
♠ A J 3	♠ K 10 5
♡ K 9 4 2	♡ A Q J 8 5
◇ A J 7 6	◇ K 10 9 8
♣ A 5	♣ 3

As dealer I opened one notrump and P.O. responded two clubs, which was doubled. I bid two hearts and P.O. countered with four clubs.

Having discussed our methods for roughly fifteen minutes prior to game time, I decided this was Gerber. P.O. said later he was prepared to have me think it was either Gerber, a splinter, or a cue bid. As we had decided to play Roman Key Card Blackwood, I responded four hearts showing one or four key cards. I hoped this wouldn't sound like a signoff.

P.O. thought I had poor trumps and was signing off. He now bid four notrump. Well, I thought, I've already shown four key cards but what the hell, I'll show four more. I responded five diamonds, once again showing one or four key cards. He now signed off in five hearts, thinking I had one ace.

Having already shown eight key cards I was not about to play in less than a slam. I concluded the scientific auction with six hearts. Now to the play.

West (me)	East (P.O.)
♠ A J 3	♠ K 10 5
♡ K 9 4 2	♡ A Q J 8 5
◊ A J 7 6	◊ K 10 9 8
♣ A 5	♣ 3

I won the club lead, drew trumps in two rounds, and ruffed a club in dummy. I continued with the ace and jack of diamonds. When North played low I rose with the king, catching air, and exited with a diamond. The opponents had to lead a spade (or give me a ruff and a sluff) and I made six hearts.

Later it was pointed out that I had misplayed the slam. At matchpoints I should finesse the diamond giving myself the best chance to make seven.

Even if the finesse loses, but my opponent has the doubleton queen of diamonds, he will be endplayed. Furthermore, if North had started with queen fourth of diamonds, I would still have had to guess the spade queen after playing ace-king of diamonds.

My excuse was that I was so exhausted after having shown eight key cards that I could not be expected to find the best play.

Reprieve

THE SETTING IS the semi-final round of the prestigious Rei-singer National Championships in Nashville, Tennessee.

This afternoon we are playing ten three-board matches for a total of thirty boards. Twenty-one teams are struggling to qualify for the final round where the field will be cut to only ten teams.

I am playing with my favorite partner, Alan Sontag. We are playing the third and final board of round four, and there are still seventeen minutes left on the clock.

To anybody else this would mean that the last hand could be played at a leisurely pace; but as a man with ulterior motives, I wish to get the hand over with quickly, or at least to be the dummy.

Why? Well, in the lobby of the hotel, not far from the playing area, my beloved Los Angeles Lakers are playing the Detroit Pistons on National Television. If I can just get this hand out of the way, I can run out and catch ten or fifteen minutes of the game. A ticket to heaven.

Alan is the dealer and opens one notrump, next hand passes, and I am looking at: ♠ Q 9 8 3 2 ♡ K 10 8 4 ◊ 7 4 ♣ A 2.

I am beside myself with joy. Given our system, there is no way I can become the declarer, and if the opponents shut up, I will be the dummy and my right hand kibitzer can play my cards for me. (I have no left hand kibitzer.)

Double-checking my hand: ♠ Q 9 8 3 2 ♡ K 10 8 4 ◊ 7 4 ♣ A 2,
I respond two clubs, Stayman, and Alan rebids two diamonds,
denying a four-card major. In my haste to get to the television, I
temporarily forget that we are playing Forcing Stayman, which
means that any major suit I now bid at the two level is forcing.

In addition, we play that the responder bids his shorter major,
showing five cards in the other major. This allows the strong hand
to declare in the five-card suit, if he has three cards in that suit
and chooses to play there.

To make a long story short, my proper bid now is two hearts,
forcing, showing exactly five spades and probably four hearts.

Thinking I am playing Non-Forcing Stayman, I rebid *three*
hearts (with Non-Forcing Stayman one must *jump* in the shorter
major to show the hand described above, this being the "Smolen"
convention). Little do I realize what I have done. I have just made
one of our "wonder" bids showing a singleton heart, four spades,
and five-three in the minors!

In fact, we had just gone over the sequence the night before;
but when the Lakers are playing, I am not at my best unless I am
actually watching the game.

Alan rebids four clubs, asking me for my five-card minor. I
think he is cue-bidding with a spade fit. However, the fact that I
have the ace of clubs bothers me slightly.

Well, I know I'm not interested in a slam but I don't want to
sign-off in four spades because then I would have to play the hand
and miss more of the game.

I invent a bid of four hearts. I am going to tell Alan this was
the way we decided to retransfer back to four spades. In fact, I am
going to tell him that it was his idea to retransfer. (Whenever you
want to avoid a lecture, simply tell your partner that the crazy bid
you have just made was his idea.)

Please Alan, bid four spades so I can watch the game. With all
the alerts, we have already wasted four precious minutes bidding
a baby hand.

Alan bids five clubs.

Dear God, is this happening to me? What is he doing? He
can't be cue-bidding again. Actually, he is bidding five clubs to
play because my previous four-heart bid showed five clubs. At this
point, you might like to see the hand. Keep in mind the bidding
isn't over, and one of the players is extremely nervous.

```
                        North (me)
                        ♠ Q 9 8 3 2
                        ♡ K 10 8 4
                        ◇ 7 4
                        ♣ A 2
        West                              East
        ♠ 7 6                             ♠ K J 4
        ♡ A Q 9 5 2                       ♡ 3
        ◇ 10 6                            ◇ K 9 8 5 2
        ♣ 9 7 6 3                         ♣ Q 10 8 4
                        South (Alan)
                        ♠ A 10 5
                        ♡ J 7 6
                        ◇ A Q J 3
                        ♣ K J 5
```

South	West	North	East
1 NT	pass	2 ♣	pass
2 ◇	pass	3 ♡	pass
4 ♣	pass	4 ♡	pass
5 ♣	pass	?	

How can I get out of this? I finally decide that his four club and five club bids are some form of Roman Key Card Blackwood. If so, my four heart response has shown three key cards and now he is asking me for kings! (Twelve minutes on the clock.)

Well, I'm not going to show him my king, so I respond five hearts which, with the responses we were using (his idea), would show no kings.

Alan thinks that my five heart bid is a cue bid heading for a slam. He cue-bids five spades. Thank God, Alan finally bid spades! I am delirious with joy. My "PASS" card practically rips a hole in the table. The bidding is over and there are still eleven minutes on the clock.

Now the opponents want an explanation of the bidding. Alan says, "Two clubs was Forcing Stayman, three hearts showed a singleton heart with five-three in the minors. Four clubs asked for his minor and four hearts said it was clubs. Five clubs was to play and five hearts and five spades were cue bids.

"Of course, he doesn't have any of that. He has four hearts, five spades, and has forgotten yet another convention."

What to do? I want to see how bad the carnage is going to be. I also want to watch the game, but no way can I desert Alan at this point. Besides, he plays most hands faster than anybody in the world. I decide to give him one minute. (Maybe they are showing a commercial during a time-out.)

```
                        North (me)
                        ♠ Q 9 8 3 2
                        ♡ K 10 8 4
                        ◇ 7 4
                        ♣ A 2
West                                            East
♠ 7 6                                           ♠ K J 4
♡ A Q 9 5 2                                     ♡ 3
◇ 10 6                                          ◇ K 9 8 5 2
♣ 9 7 6 3                                       ♣ Q 10 8 4
                        South (Alan)
                        ♠ A 10 5
                        ♡ J 7 6
                        ◇ A Q J 3
                        ♣ K J 5
```

The opening lead is the ten of diamonds which Alan wins with the queen. He crosses to the ace of clubs and successfully runs the spade nine. He wins the second spade with the ace, leads a heart to the ten, finesses the diamond, and leads another heart to West's ace. All the opponents can take are a heart and a spade, making five in 39 seconds!

East is beside himself because he could have defeated the contract by splitting his spade honors in order to get a heart ruff.

I, on the other hand, am overjoyed. I don't even mind when Alan says (as I am dashing out), "We have cut our important conventions down to only four, and you have already forgotten two."

"You're right, Alan. I did forget, but you made the hand and I love you."

P.S. The Lakers lost.

P.P.S. So did we in the finals.

V
Women in My Life

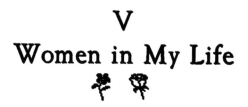

And Then I Got Married

UNLESS ONE ACTUALLY does it, one cannot understand the enormous psychological factors involved when marrying another bridge player. The urge to impress the love of your life is rather strong if you know what I mean.

Early in my marriage (it would have to be early as I was only married a little over a year) to Phyllis we sauntered over to the plush Savoy Bridge Club in Los Angeles, and I immediately cut into the high stake game. Phyllis was kibitzing with watchful eyes, if you know what I mean.

It wasn't too long before this hand came up. Both sides were vulnerable and my partner, Kai Larsen, was the dealer:

North (Larsen)
♠ 10 7 3
♡ A K Q 9 3
◊ A 10 5 4
♣ 7

West (George Bassman)
♠ K 8 6 4
♡ 5
◊ 8 6 2
♣ Q 10 5 4 2

East (Lew Mathe)
♠ A 9 2
♡ 10 8 6 4 2
◊ Q 9 7
♣ A 3

South (me)
♠ Q J 5
♡ J 7
◊ K J 3
♣ K J 9 8 6

Southwest (Phyllis)

Kai opened one heart and I responded two notrump. I had to show Phyllis right off I was no point counter, and while others may need 13-15 to respond two notrump, I could get by with twelve.

Kai rebid three diamonds and my confident three notrump ended the auction. George led the club four and I could hardly resist a sideways glance when I got this lead into my oh-so-cleverly concealed five-card suit.

Mathe, one of the club's owners, won the ace and, after a moment of reflection, shifted to the spade deuce. I tried the queen, Bassman won the king and continued with the spade eight! I played low from dummy, Mathe played the spade nine and I won the jack.

The hand did not appear to be difficult. It seemed I had oodles of tricks. I played the jack of hearts and a second heart. When Bassman discarded a club, my oodles had suddenly become eight.

Oh well, great players don't let bad breaks bother them. Besides, Phyllis was watching me, checking on my composure. Fortunately, she couldn't see my Southeast perspiration from her Southwest chair.

Stalling, I played a third heart, discarding a club, while Bassman discarded a diamond.

It looked to me like George had started with five or six clubs, three spades, one heart and either three or four diamonds. For a great player I have the curious habit of misguessing queens, so rather than take the diamond finesse one way or the other, I exited with a spade from dummy, cleverly unblocking their spade suit.

The possibility that Bassman had four spades, I admit, never crossed my mind. Who returns the spade eight from ♠ K-8-6-4?

Mathe won the ace and took a little while to consider the position. He couldn't fool me, I "knew" he was afraid to cash his fourth spade for fear of squeezing George in the minors. Who did he think he was playing against anyway?

As I suspected, he exited with a club. Don't worry Lew, I'm on to your game, and Phyllis, are you watching? At this point I had the K-J-3 of diamonds and the K-J-9 of clubs and had lost three tricks. What could be sweeter? On Mathe's club shift, I would simply pass the club nine into Bassman's hand and wait for the minor suit return which would insure my ninth trick.

I couldn't resist the grand gesture. When I played the club nine, I tabled my cards and announced, "George, you're endplayed for my ninth trick."

"By God, you're right," said George as he cashed the spade six for the setting trick.

Come to think of it, how did I stay married so long?

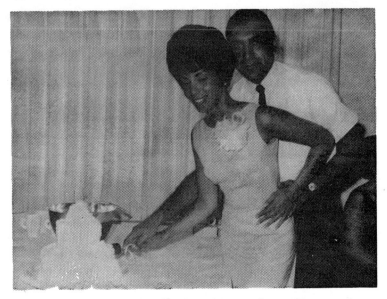

Phyllis and I cutting the cake—not the cards.

With Phyllis and my parents, Alice and Sigmund.

My Father's Son
— the Bridge Teacher

EARLY IN LIFE I decided I would either have to work for a living or enjoy myself. Observation showed that very few people could combine both. I decided to enjoy myself. I became a bridge teacher.

I have been teaching bridge for the past 17 years, steadily for the past six or seven. I can just see Stoney wince as he reads this. He is not feeling sorry for me, mind you, but for the people I've been teaching.

You see, Stoney thinks I can barely follow suit. But that's not really an insult. Stoney thinks only five people in the world can play bridge, and he's not fully convinced about the other four.

Incidentally, Alvin Roth and Tobias Stone have thoroughly indoctrinated their followers in the theory that five-card majors are the only way to play. If I ever happen to get a decent result against a Roth-Stoner by opening a four-card major, he invariably takes my hand out of the board. He and his partner examine my four-card suit as though it were some kind of snake.

However, for all of Stone's conversation, Roth makes him look like a piker. In Toronto, when Marshall Miles and I played (and I use the term generously) on the same knockout team with them, Roth would inspire confidence in Marshall and me by making a plane reservation home before each match.

I only mention this because I teach my classes to open four-card majors, if the hand calls for it, and I wanted the five-card majorites to know this before reading on. Four-card major propaganda may be on their banned reading list.

Oh yes, I also teach them to count for long suits instead of short ones when originally evaluating their hands. I would estimate conservatively that this has cost me close to three years of my life in futile explanations. (Many of my ladies sneak Goren books into class.)

I once mentioned that in order to give your partner a double raise you need at least four trumps and 13-16 points in support of partner's suit. Suddenly a woman began leafing through her Goren book. She looked at the woman she came with, and with obvious relief, said, "He's going to be all right—he tells the truth!"

Now that I am in my declining years I have recklessly begun to teach limit raises. Live it up, and let the chips fall where they may.

I started out, naively enough, by teaching beginners. I should have realized immediately that I was not cut out for this. In one of my first classes I walked over to help someone play a hand. After a few tricks every single card in the dummy was good and there was no way, even for this lady, to lose another trick. I simply said, "Go over to the dummy and take the rest of the tricks." With that, I left to assist at another table. As I glanced back I saw the lady walking around the table to get over to the dummy!

At times they call me over to the table. "What should I play now?" the declarer usually asks me. I take a look and see six cards in everybody's hand. "What's trump?" I ask, stalling for time. "Hearts." "Do they have any left?" "One or two, but only little ones." "Are those clubs in dummy good?" "I don't remember, it's been a long time since they were played. Esther, are those clubs in dummy good?" "How should I know? I'm not playing the hand."

Sometimes they come and tell me about a hand they played at home the night before. "I was playing with my husband," the story usually begins (she's clearly looking for sympathy, but she forgets I'm on *his* side), "and he bid three spades. What should I have done?"

"You mean he opened three spades?"

"No, I bid one heart, he gave me one spade, I gave him three clubs." (This is a very generous game.) "And he mentioned three spades. What should I have done?"

"Do you remember your hand?"

"Oh yes, my hand. I had no spades, or maybe one, the queen, king, ten, ace, nine and an x in hearts—like you put on the board—the king of diamonds with some others, and the rest clubs, but it doesn't matter. Anyway, I said four hearts and he said we could have made three notrump. Was he right?"

"No," I say, hating myself, but business is slow and I can't afford to lose anybody. "You were right. You had an automatic four heart bid."

The last straw came up a few years ago when I was teaching the fifth lesson of a series for beginners. This particular lady came to class thinking it was the first lesson, and she just happened to sit South. I had a prepared hand on the table, open-faced, and was about to explain the bidding. I began by saying that South was the dealer and that with 14 points and a five-card spade suit—in beginning classes you give them at least five-card suits or they won't bid at all—the correct opening was one spade.

"Mr. Kantar," this woman said, raising her hand, "*which* spade should I bid?"

After a bit you get to recognize questions of this type. If you try to answer them you usually wind up wishing you *had* gone to work for a living. I parried, "Why don't you wait a bit and you'll see what the bidding means." She seemed satisfied, so I continued: "South opens one spade . . ." "Mr. Kantar, where should I put the spade?"

Well, I answered that question and that is why I no longer teach "beginning" classes. I now call my classes "intermediate" and "advanced." The fact that the same people come does not disturb me.

In all of these classes I start out by giving a 20 to 40-minute lecture on the topic of the day and then call out prepared hands for distribution at the tables. Each player takes a suit, and I call off one suit at a time. Using this method I can teach any number of tables without trouble—provided everyone distributes the cards properly.

The fact that "eight" and "ace" sound so much alike has caused endless confusion, to say nothing of those students who forget to distribute the suit they are holding, to say nothing of the fact that somebody always winds up with too many or too few cards, to say nothing of the fact that almost no one bothers to count his cards, to say nothing of my mistakes as I call the cards. Otherwise, it is an infallible system.

In one of my "beginning" classes (which I had been teaching for about five years) a truly memorable event occurred. Having called out the hands, I noticed that one lady had wound up with 20 cards and her partner six. True to their code of trusting me implicitly, it didn't seem to faze either of them.

The lady with the 20 cards was one of my better students; by that I mean she had decided to go all-out and count for long suits, regardless of what certain books said. She was trying to count up her hand, but her real problem was in trying to hold on to her cards. She needed a basket; they kept falling. Finally she got organized, and with her 6-8-4-2 distribution she came through admirably with a one heart opening. Next hand passed, and her partner was in a quandary.

This was an older woman, who had counted for short suits all her life, and she wasn't going to let a young upstart change her bidding habits. Relying on her years of experience, she realized that with her 0-1-3-2 distribution she had a truly magnificent hand. Why, in short suits alone she practically had an opening bid! I was finally called over and revealed all. But it hurt.

Some women have been so overcome with my teaching that they can't wait to tell me how much they got out of one of the lessons. A little while back a lady came up to me after class and said that the lesson I had given the week before on redoubles had really helped her.

She proceeded to tell me about a recent hand. "My right-hand opponent opened one heart and I doubled. Next player passed, and my partner redoubled—just as you said, because she had more than ten points."

Over the years, one tries not to repeat the same mistakes. The error I keep making is trying to teach them which card to lead, especially in partner's suit. I know and they know that they are going to lead the highest card, whatever I say, but they are very polite while I'm explaining.

Third hand play is one of my favorite lessons because it gives me a chance to ask questions like this:

```
                        North
                        x x x
        West                            East
        Q x x x x                       J
                        South
                        A
```

I ask them (after sufficient explanation) to pretend that they are West, defending a notrump contract. "Assume," I say, "you lead a low card and your partner plays the jack, which loses to declarer's ace. Who has the king?" (That, of course, is a pretty tough one for the class, but I am ruthless.)

Aside from the few who think it is in the dummy (possibly hidden under an x), most students, who believe that false-carding amounts to cheating, will answer "East." The bright ones always say "South," but I once had a lady who liked to play safe. Her answer was "Southeast."

As I mentioned earlier, I enjoy my work and I even teach a few people to play. Take the lady who, as declarer, would never attack a suit in which she didn't have the ace and king. Finally I forced her (by wrenching the card from her hand) to lead up to a king-jack combination in dummy. I carefully explained that it was simply a guess; if she thought the ace was on her left, to play the king, and if she thought it was on her right, to play the jack. I went through it again, then asked her which one she wanted to play from dummy, and to tell me what she was hoping for when she made her play.

After indescribable agony, she finally played the king. "What are you hoping for?" I asked. "I'm hoping they make a mistake," was the profound reply.

Valerie, one of my first students.
No wonder I love to teach bridge.

With Valerie in London. (No, I'm not
on the horse! I'm taking the picture.)

Ceci and Me

I MET CECI three months ago and life has just not been the same, nor will it probably ever be.

Aside from everything else, Ceci adores playing bridge almost as much as she adores her cuddly Maltese, Minny, who kibitzes our games regularly with a lapside view. Throw in the sun (she is an avid sun-worshipper) and you will begin to get the idea of where I fit into the picture. At the moment I am a distant fourth and losing ground rapidly.

The only way I can possibly make it to third is to pick up some Master Points for Ceci. You see winning isn't the only thing to Ceci, it is everything. Ask her how many points she has and she will answer, "Oh, who keeps track? About 80.53."

Now for a word or two about Ceci's game before I met her. She never had any formal instruction and played by the seat of her pants with pretty good results. Ceci is a lucky player. No matter what she does she somehow manages to fall on her feet while both her opponents and her partner look at one another in amazement.

Now that I have entered the picture and tried to discipline her game a bit, one can understand the trying times we are going through.

The hardest thing for me to do is to try to explain to Ceci, after one of her incredible bids has just given us another top, that perhaps it wasn't the best of all possible actions.

For example, her conception of the penalty double has either advanced or set *my* game back some twenty odd years.

To give you an idea, Ceci believes the best penalty doubles are made when you have a fit in your partner's suit, and not too many of the opponents' trumps. This idea seemed rather wild to me at first, but as time went by, I began to see the infinite wisdom of it.

West dealer
Both sides vulnerable

```
                        North
                        ♠ 10 7 6
                        ♡ 10 9 8
                        ◇ J 9 8 5
                        ♣ 10 8 2
        West                            East
        ♠ A K 9 2                       ♠ J 4 3
        ♡ A K Q                         ♡ J 7 6 5 2
        ◇ Q 10 7 6 3                    ◇ A 4
        ♣ J                             ♣ A 9 5
                        South
                        ♠ Q 8 5
                        ♡ 4 3
                        ◇ K 2
                        ♣ K Q 7 6 4 3
```

Ceci		*Me*	
West	North	East	South
1 ◇	pass	1 ♡	2 ♣
double!	(all pass)		

Opening lead: ♡ K

Strangely enough, when most experts were given Ceci's hand as a rebid problem, not one found the "obvious" double. After three rounds of hearts, declarer could come up with no more than five trump tricks, and went down 800 peacefully.

Tactfully, I mentioned to Ceci that perhaps her trump holding left a little to be desired for such a low-level penalty double. She nodded. Only a few days later did I understand the full significance of that nod.

East dealer
Both sides vulnerable

North
♠ 10 8 6
♡ 8 7 6 3
◊ 9 2
♣ K J 9 3

West
♠ K 9 4 2
♡ —
◊ K J 7 6 3
♣ A 8 4 2

East
♠ Q 7 5
♡ A J
◊ A Q 8 4
♣ Q 10 7 5

South
♠ A J 3
♡ K Q 10 9 5 4 2
◊ 10 5
♣ 6

West	North	East	South
—	—	1 NT	3 ♡
double!	(all pass)		

Opening lead: ♠ 2

Guess who doubled. Of course, the hand was defeated one trick, and we have no game, so all explanation was futile. However, now that I think of it, Ceci and I have a private understanding which we do not put on our convention cards. When Ceci doubles for penalties she denies trump length. When she does have their suit, she bids notrump. Ah well, no wonder I wasn't winning anything until I met her.

To further compound this madness, Ceci tried it my way twice and doubled for penalties when she had four and five trumps. They made it both times and, as inevitable as death and taxes, came, "You see what happens when you have too many trumps—they get in your way."

To try to stop Ceci from underleading aces against suit contracts is equally fruitless.

North dealer
Both sides vulnerable

                          North
                          ♠ 7 6 5 4
                          ♡ K J 8
                          ♦ K 4
                          ♣ K 7 6 5

        West   East
        ♠ 10   ♠ A 9 8
        ♡ A 9 7 5 2   ♡ Q 10 6 4 3
        ♦ 9 8 5 2   ♦ A 3
        ♣ Q 10 4   ♣ 9 8 2

                          South
                          ♠ K Q J 3 2
                          ♡ —
                          ♦ Q J 10 7 6
                          ♣ A J 3

Ceci		*Me*	
West	North	East	South
—	pass	pass	1 ♠
pass	3 ♠	pass	4 ♠
(all pass)			

Opening lead: ♡ 5

After all, what else would one lead on this bidding? Declarer woodenly played the jack and ruffed my queen. The king of spades was taken by the ace and a heart returned. If declarer ruffs, he must later lose either a heart or a trump trick (by being forced to ruff a third heart with an honor), so he discarded. We were the only pair in the room to hold declarer to four.

Not having had enough success by underleading five to the ace, Ceci was now playing against the same declarer a few days later.

East dealer
East-West vulnerable

	North	
	♠ 10 8 4 2	
	♡ A J 10 5	
	◊ A J 5	
	♣ K Q	

West		East
♠ K		♠ A J 9 5
♡ 9 8 6		♡ K Q 3
◊ 10 9 7		◊ 6 2
♣ A 10 8 6 4 3		♣ J 9 7 5

	South	
	♠ Q 7 6 3	
	♡ 7 4 2	
	◊ K Q 8 4 3	
	♣ 2	

Ceci		*Me*	
West	North	East	South
—	—	pass	pass
pass	1 ◊	double	1 ♠
pass!	2 ♠	(all pass)	

When I asked Ceci later why she didn't mention her clubs, she said that if she bid them and everyone passed, she would have had to play the hand. For a moment I had completely forgotten how Ceci's mind works.

Anyway if you don't bid a six-card suit headed by the ace-ten, you surely lead it—I mean you surely underlead it! The opening lead was the six of clubs. Notice the honesty. Always fourth best.

Too bad the K-J doubleton wasn't in dummy, but declarer won the first trick and led a trump. I played low and declarer, placing me with the ace-king of spades, played the queen. Ceci won the king and hopefully laid down the ace of clubs which declarer ruffed. I said nothing nor did I look at Ceci. (You will learn why later.)

Slightly bewildered by this turn of events, declarer led another trump. I then drew all of the remaining trumps and we ran our club suit to defeat the hand three tricks.

After the hand, declarer, still fuming, asked Ceci if she always underleads aces. "Only when I have them," was the reply.

One of the main reasons my position in Ceci's affections is a losing fourth is that my behavior at the bridge table is not always optimum. For example, if I violate any of the following rules (commandments), there is no telling how far downward I might spiral.

RULES FOR EDWIN TO REMEMBER WHEN PLAYING WITH CECI

1. Always, but always, look at any dummy Ceci puts down with love and affection, no matter how hideous it might really be.

2. Never, never say a cross word or give anything but adoring looks across the table no matter how much the urge to "kill" surges from within.

3. Never concede the rest of the tricks to the opponents even though declarer has seven cards remaining—six high trumps and an ace—and Ceci has a small trump. Somehow, declarer might forget about Ceci's deuce and she might be able to trump that ace.

4. No matter how many suits Ceci bids, it does not necessarily mean that she has a distributional hand. It just means that she wants me to bid the notrump. "For God's sake, I thought you were *never* going to bid it."

5. Get the best possible teammates for any local event even if it means making a long distance call to Rome for Garozzo and Belladonna.

6. Win!

We have yet to cover Ceci's play of the hand or her slam bidding. Here is an example of what goes on in my mind when I watch Ceci play a hand.

North dealer
North-South vulnerable

```
                            North
                            ♠ —
                            ♡ A K 9 3
                            ◊ J 7 6 3 2
                            ♣ Q J 10 7
        West                                East
        ♠ J 6 2                             ♠ Q 8 7 5 4 3
        ♡ 10 4                              ♡ Q J 8 7
        ◊ K 5                               ◊ A 9 4
        ♣ K 9 8 6 3 2                       ♣ —
                            South
                            ♠ A K 10 9
                            ♡ 6 5 2
                            ◊ Q 10 8
                            ♣ A 5 4
```

	Me		*Ceci*
West	North	East	South
—	pass	1 ♠	pass
2 ♠	double	pass	2 NT
pass	3 ◊	3 ♠	3 NT
(all pass)			

Another logical auction with Ceci. I couldn't stand two notrump so, naturally, Ceci bid three notrump. And, of course, she doesn't double three spades; so I know she must be loaded in that suit.

Anyway, a spade is led and I figure that Ceci must have a big diamond fit with me (if I were playing with Marshall Miles, I would bet that he had at least five diamonds) and is counting on running that suit.

Ceci's first discard from the dummy is a diamond. Wrong again! The next card out of her hand is the queen of diamonds! First she discards one, then she plays one . . . . Dear God, I must be going crazy. I must stop worrying about what she is doing because it almost always works out.

When the smoke cleared, Ceci had made four notrump and was beaming. (The jack of spades was led—we were playing in a tough field—and doubling three spades would hardly have been worthwhile as declarer can get out for down one.)

Without giving you a full description of another hand Ceci played, I must tell you about her management of a suit combination.

North (me)
◇ A K Q 4 3

West
◇ 9 5

East
◇ J 8 6 2

South (Ceci)
◇ 10 7

Ceci was playing a heart partial and diamonds was dummy's first bid suit. West led the nine of diamonds. My attention wandered for a moment and later, as I looked down at the trick, I saw that Ceci had called a low diamond from dummy and had won the trick with the ten!

Now I was angry at myself for not steering the hand to my beloved notrump, as Ceci apparently had the jack and ten of diamonds—even though I had mentioned (sweetly) that she should win these tricks with the higher of equal cards.

As Ceci pondered the dummy (a rarity), I glanced into my left hand opponent's hand (soon to be another no-no), and lo and behold, there was the jack of diamonds!

Mixed emotions set in. At least Ceci had not forgotten about taking tricks with the higher of equals; but how in blazes did she make her ten of diamonds, why did she duck, and how come East (a competent player) still had the jack of diamonds?

It developed that Ceci meant to call for a high diamond but she said small instead. East was so sure she was going to call for a high diamond that he also ducked, and at least that mystery was solved.

I hate to add this, but later in the hand Ceci played off two high diamonds and West ruffed. West in turn put her partner back in to play the jack of diamonds, and although I'm not sure, I think Ceci finally wound up losing an extra trick by ducking the diamond lead in the first place.

Ceci is not beneath taking an occasional practice finesse if the situation demands it. The definition of a practice finesse is (in case you are interested) a finesse which, if it works, gives you the same number of tricks you would have taken if you had not finessed at all. But it does keep you in practice.

North dealer
East-West vulnerable

```
                        North
                        ♠ J 10 6 5
                        ♡ K J 10 9 8 7
                        ◇ 5
                        ♣ Q 7
        West                                East
        ♠ 7 3                               ♠ A 8
        ♡ Q 6 5                             ♡ 3 2
        ◇ K 10 8 7                          ◇ A J 4 3
        ♣ A 10 6 2                          ♣ K 9 8 5 4
                        South
                        ♠ K Q 9 4 2
                        ♡ A 4
                        ◇ Q 9 6 2
                        ♣ J 3
```

	Me		*Ceci*
West	North	East	South
—	pass	pass	1 ♠
pass	3 ♠	(all pass)	

Opening lead: ♠ 3

East won the trick and returned a club to West's ace. West played another trump thus giving Ceci a chance to do a little "practicing."

Notice that if Ceci plays the ace-king and a third heart, ruffing, she can then get back to dummy with a trump, discard a club and two diamonds on the hearts and concede a diamond to make four.

However, the more aesthetic way to make four is to play the ace and finesse the jack of hearts. Now if the finesse loses, you are down one, but if it works you get rid of one club and three diamonds and still make four.

Ceci took the finesse ("West could have had four hearts, Edwin darling"). Naturally it worked, and naturally we got a good result. Most of the pairs were in four going down one—which Ceci was quick to point out to me as she gazed at the other scores on the pickup slip.

Ceci has recently given me another rule which states in no uncertain terms that we must bid any slam that makes. This, in turn, puts a little (just a little, mind you) pressure on me who, even without these ultimatums, has a tough enough time on slams.

It turns out Ceci and I missed a good seven hearts on these two hands, which cost us a Swiss Team match.

Dealer (Ceci)	Third Hand (Me)
♠ 4 2	♠ A Q 10 9 5
♡ A K 8 7 4 3	♡ Q 6
◇ A K Q 6 5	◇ J 10
♣ —	♣ A Q 9 4
1 ♡	1 ♠
3 ◇	3 ♡
4 ♡	4 NT
5 ♡	5 NT
6 ♡	6 NT
pass	

With the hearts breaking three-two, there was no problem in the play. We had missed a grand slam and that was not so good.

Then this one came up shortly thereafter:

Dealer (Ceci)		Third Hand (Me)
♠ Q 5 4 3		♠ —
♡ A Q 10 6 5 4		♡ J 9 2
◇ 5 4		◇ A K 7 3
♣ 3		♣ A K Q 8 4 2
pass		1 ♣
1 ♡	(1 ♠)	2 ◇
2 ♡		2 ♠
3 ♠ !		5 ♡
pass		

The opening lead was the king of spades. Making seven with the heart finesse onside.

Well, this called for a little discussion. It turned out that my spade cue bid had confused her and her spade raise had scared her. That is why we did not reach the slam, although we did agree that my jump to five was asking about the quality of her trump suit.

So that was two slams down the tubes and even Minny was getting restless watching this ineptitude. Then came this number:

East dealer
North-South vulnerable

```
                    North
                    ♠ A
                    ♡ 7 6
                    ◇ 10 5 4
                    ♣ A 10 9 6 5 3 2
        West                        East
        ♠ K J 9 5 4 3 2             ♠ 10 7 6
        ♡ 8                         ♡ A J 10 5 4 3
        ◇ 7 6 3                     ◇ J 8 2
        ♣ J 4                       ♣ Q
                    South
                    ♠ Q 8
                    ♡ K Q 9 2
                    ◇ A K Q 9
                    ♣ K 8 7
```

	Ceci		*Me*
West	North	East	South
—	—	2 ♡ (weak)	3 NT

At this point West asked Ceci what my three notrump bid meant. Ceci answered that it was forcing to game. West passed and Ceci leaped to six notrump, the only slam that makes. A heart ruff will beat any suit slam.

But our very best hand was the following:

North dealer
East-West vulnerable

North
♠ A K Q 7 6
♡ —
◇ 6 5 3
♣ Q 8 7 6 4

South
♠ 5 3
♡ 7 6 3
◇ K J 4
♣ A K J 9 3

Me		*Ceci*
North		South
1 ♠ *		2 ♣
3 ♣		3 ◇
3 ♡	(double)	4 ♣ **
6 ♣		(all pass)

* In my book I recommend opening these minimum five-five black hands with one club; but that book was written before I met Ceci and she has altered my bidding style somewhat.

** At this point West asked Ceci about the meaning of my three heart bid. Ceci's answer would have gladdened the heart of any partner. "Oh, he's either asking me or telling me something, I don't know which, and I don't care."

A heart was led. Ceci ruffed, drew trumps in two rounds, and set up the spades (they were 4-2) for two diamond discards, to make a slam with only 23 high card points between the combined hands.

Who knows, maybe I will get to third place one of these days.

My Home Game

MY FEW REMAINING FANS may be wondering why they haven't seen my name in the winner's circle much in the past few years. After mulling the problem over, I have come up with at least two reasons (excuses) for my current demise:

(1) My regular partner, Alan Sontag, lives in New York City, and we play together only three or four times a year.

(2) The home game I have been playing in regularly for the past five years.

Since Alan is a wonderful player, I can only conclude that it must be the home game. Let me tell you a little about the players and then show you a representative hand. The lineup:

—Judy. Former girlfriend who is so thrilled she got rid of me that she still has me over for dinner at least once a week. These dinners are followed by bridge. Judy is a ticket agent for American Airlines, and she currently gets up at 4:30 a.m. (This is relevant.)

—Roy, her husband, very bright and, if not the nicest guy in the world, must rank in the top ten on anybody's list. When Judy reflects on this, I sometimes get invited to dinner twice a week.

—Yvonne, my girlfriend. Bilingual schoolteacher and mother of two. Yvonne used to enjoy bridge before she met me, before she was introduced to such awful terms as *thinking, remembering, signalling* and, worst of all, *counting.*

I have tried to shape this game up (terrorize it) in a number of ways. I badger both Roy and Judy to be more aggressive in the bidding, and ask them questions during the play and defense to keep them *thinking bridge.* As for Yvonne, she has a tendency (compulsion) to overcall on moth-infested four-card suits. On the plus side, whenever she makes a penalty double, both Roy and Judy shiver.

At one time or another I have noticed each of the players heave a sigh of relief when they are dummy, knowing that the inquisition is over for the moment.

The level of the game is actually improving (it had to), but then again, every so often something happens such as I am about to describe.

It might be helpful to tell you a bit about the *previous* hand. Judy had preempted in spades, and Yvonne became declarer in four clubs. Roy led the ace of spades. They play suit preference signals by the preemptor, and Judy, holding the ace of diamonds and a heart void, played the spade two, asking for a diamond. (She should have signalled for a heart.)

Roy shifted to a heart. Judy ruffed, underled her diamond ace to Roy's king and ruffed another heart. She then cashed the diamond ace to put us two down.

They were happy with this result. I couldn't bear to see all this glee go by without making a few cutting remarks.

For openers I did not tell them they could make four spades. I may be mean, but I'm not cruel. Besides, Yvonne doesn't like it if I say anything sarcastic.

"Judy, why did you play the two of spades?"

"I had the ace of diamonds and wanted Roy to shift to a diamond."

"What about your heart void?"

"I forgot I was void in hearts; I got up very early this morning."

At this point Yvonne nodded in understanding. She also gets up early. Yvonne always understands and agrees with Judy's explanations. A soul sister, so to speak.

"Roy, why did you shift to a heart after partner asked you for a diamond?"

"Because I had five hearts, dummy had five and Judy hasn't had much sleep today."

With that as a background, let's look at the *hand of the evening*. Let it be known that I have asked for written releases from the other players so I could write this hand up. (None were given.)

North dealer
Both sides stuffed with a great dinner

```
                        North (Me)
                        ♠ K 10 8 7
                        ♡ 2
                        ◇ J 8
                        ♣ A Q J 10 3 2
        West (Roy)                      East (Judy)
        ♠ 3                             ♠ Q J 9 6 2
        ♡ A 9 8 7                       ♡ K 10 6 3
        ◇ K Q 10 5 4                    ◇ 3 2
        ♣ 9 8 7                         ♣ 5 4
                        South (Yvonne)
                        ♠ A 5 4
                        ♡ Q J 5 4
                        ◇ A 9 7 6
                        ♣ K 6
```

Roy	*Me*	*Judy*	*Yvonne*
West	North	East	South
—	1 ♣	pass	1 ♡ [1]
pass	1 ♠	pass	2 NT
pass	3 ♣ [2]	pass	3 ♡
pass	3 NT	(all pass)	

[1] Had her diamond ace in with her hearts. Had she seen the hand as it actually was, she probably would have responded two notrump. She saves these types of four-card suits for her overcalls.

[2] Prepared to tell Yvonne that three clubs was forcing if she passed and we missed game; or that three clubs was not forcing if she bid on and we went down. (My word has been law in this game—until this article appeared.)

Opening lead: ◇ K

As I began to put the dummy down, clubs and diamonds first, Yvonne, who never, *ever* says anything when she sees dummy, blurted out, "I don't believe this."

North (Me)
♠ K 10 8 7
♡ 2
◇ J 8
♣ A Q J 10 3 2

West (Roy)
♠ 3
♡ A 9 8 7
◇ K Q 10 5 4
♣ 9 8 7

East (Judy)
♠ Q J 9 6 2
♡ K 10 6 3
◇ 3 2
♣ 5 4

South (Yvonne)
♠ A 5 4
♡ Q J 5 4
◇ A 9 7 6
♣ K 6

I couldn't figure out what she was talking about. She hadn't seen my major suit cards, so how could she possibly know I was a little on the light side?

It turned out, of course, that she thought she had three little diamonds, and that I had bid notrump without a diamond stopper. She forgot she had bid notrump first.

Now for the play (?). The diamond king and queen both held, and Roy continued with the ten (?). Judy discarded the spade two, upside down attitude (we all use the modern signalling methods), and Yvonne followed with the nine.

Roy was now caught on the horns of a dilemma that could only happen in this game. Was there no ace of diamonds in this deck? Was Yvonne holding up, holding up and holding up once again? Had Judy revoked? Was the ace of diamonds on the floor? Here I was in a game where not one of the four players knew who had the ace of diamonds.

Although the hand could now be defeated with a heart switch, Roy decided to play for the ace of diamonds to be on the floor and continued the suit. But Yvonne was ready for that play. As she was about to discard a heart rather than a spade, she discovered her ace of diamonds and quickly took her nine tricks. No big deal.

My question is: In this atmosphere, it's not possible that my game has slipped a bit, is it?

VI
Two Stories I Love

Nocturne
by Frederick B. Turner

MY BEST EXPLOITS at the bridge table occur late at night after too much rare roast beef and a superfluity of sour cream. And I don't mean a late game at the club. I mean in bed.

How many times, panting with excitement, have I awakened at 4 A.M. with the acclaim of the gallery around the VuGraph still pounding in my head? I used to keep a notebook at bedside to record for posterity an undescribed squeeze so esoteric that it left my opponents numb with bewildered frustration. The only trouble was that in the cold light of morning it was I who was bewildered. My brilliancies evaporated in a confusion of hands with five suits and 16 cards, or deals with two heart aces and no kings. And once there were five players in the game.

So, now I pretty much ignore these nocturnal fantasies. As a result, my wife no longer has to suffer through agonizing postmortems as I strive fruitlessly to recreate some nebulous midnight coup. But recently I had another one of these spells and this time, curiously enough, I could recall both the hands and associated events with frightening clarity.

In this dream, I was abroad in some large city in which the World Championship of bridge was being staged. The final match involved the Italians and the British. I don't know who had composed the American team, or why this group had fallen short of the finals. Nor do I know when these events transpired. However, things had a contemporary flavor because the players were all familiar. The Italian team was the same old six: D'Alelio, Avarelli, Belladonna, Forquet, Garozzo and Pabis-Ticci. For some reason, the British were represented by only five players: Flint, Harrison-Gray, Konstam, Reese and Schapiro.

When the finals began—on a Monday as I recall—I was amazed to find myself the only spectator in a huge auditorium designed to seat several thousand. Play began in the open room with Reese and Schapiro opposing Avarelli and Belladonna. Things went well for the English on the first day, and even better on the next. With all of the Britons in top form, the match seemed almost like a microcosmic recapitulation of the Battle of Tobruk.

With a lead of 58 IMPs, the British exuded a quiet confidence as I watched them at breakfast on Wednesday. I showed up again at game time that afternoon—once more the only spectator in the vast auditorium. When I arrived, the Italians were already at their places. Reese arrived two minutes late and obviously anxious. I was seated close enough to the table to hear what was going on.

"Schapiro's sick," Reese explained tersely. "He's probably out for the match. And I can't find Flint!"

There followed a complicated discussion with the referees and, although the Italians were sympathetic, the upshot of all the talk was that the British would have to forfeit.

I don't know what impelled my next actions, but to my astonishment I found myself on the stage volunteering to fill out the British team. Again there was much discussion, but in the end my proposal was accepted by both sides. Reese and I were to have half-an-hour together, and play would begin at 2:15 P.M. A few minutes later, in a quiet anteroom, Reese began a complex exposition of his bidding system. After a while I interrupted.

"I can't follow all this stuff about the Little Major. Let's forget the junk and just bid natural. You know, Standard American."

"Yes, I do know 'Standard American,' as you put it," Reese rejoined with what seemed almost repugnance.

"Besides," I continued with measured emphasis, "I've read your book!"

"Which book? I've—"

"Improve Your Bidding Judgment," I replied significantly. "I know every nuance of your bidding philosophy—both strategic and tactical. We can take these guys without any gimmicks."

Reese sighed and looked at his watch. "Very well. I believe it's time to begin."

We rejoined the Italians, and I was given the South seat.

"Do you know the Neapolitan Club?" Forquet asked graciously.

"No, I don't. But I've hit the Gallo di Oro and there's that funny little place in the Via—"

"I believe Signor Forquet is alluding to their bidding system," Reese observed quietly.

"Oh. Well, no. I guess I'm not familiar with that one," I confessed.

"Are you playing the Little Major?" Forquet asked Reese.

"No, we're not. Nothing unusual." Reese shrugged helplessly. Forquet and Garozzo exchanged glances.

"In that event, my partner and I have agreed to forego our normal bidding methods," said Forquet. "We'll use a natural system fairly similar to your own."

"Well, that's very sporting of you gentlemen." Reese smiled for the first time.

"Yeah, that'll make the game a lot better," I agreed. "A truer test of skill."

Reese winced and began to shuffle.

The first few boards were uneventful. True, I missed a peter and failed to give Reese a ruff in defending against two spades. This would have put them one down, but after all it was just one trick.

The sixth deal was as follows:

North dealer
North-South vulnerable

                              North
                              ♠ A K 9 7 6 3
                              ♡ —
                              ◊ A J 10 7 3
                              ♣ 8 4

West   **East**
♠ Q   ♠ J 10 5 4
♡ K 9 7   ♡ A Q 8 6 4 2
◊ 8 6 5 4   ◊ 9
♣ K Q 10 9 2   ♣ A J

                              South
                              ♠ 8 2
                              ♡ J 10 5 3
                              ◊ K Q 2
                              ♣ 7 6 5 3

Forquet	*Reese*	*Garozzo*	*Me*
West	North	East	South
—	1 ♠	2 ♡	pass
3 ♡	4 ◊	4 ♡	(all pass)

I led the king of diamonds and continued with the queen,
which Garozzo ruffed. The king of hearts was cashed and then
Garozzo passed a small heart to my ten. I led my last diamond, but
declarer ruffed and cashed the ace and queen of hearts. There
followed five rounds of club, and four hearts was made.

"Umph," Reese grunted. "We've got a fair save in four spades.
And if spades had been 3-2 I could have made game in either
spades *or* diamonds."

"True," I conceded, "but I knew the suits were going to split
badly. Besides, this hand is just like the one on page 132 of your
book. As you pointed out, to press on with my cards is the
expert's error."

"Quite right," Reese agreed. "But this time it would have saved
a few IMPs."

A few deals later, another interesting hand came up:

```
                        North
                        ♠ 7 6
                        ♡ 3
                        ◊ K Q 2
                        ♣ K J 10 9 6 5 2
        West                            East
        ♠ A 8 4 2                       ♠ Q J 10 9
        ♡ J 10 8 4                      ♡ 7 6 5
        ◊ A 10 9 4                      ◊ 8 7 6 5
        ♣ Q                            ♣ 8 4
                        South
                        ♠ K 5 3
                        ♡ A K Q 9 2
                        ◊ J 3
                        ♣ A 7 3
```

Forquet	*Reese*	*Garozzo*	*Me*
West	North	East	South
—	3 ♣	pass	3 ♡
pass	3 NT	(all pass)	

Garozzo led the spade queen and the defense took the first five tricks.

"Too bad," murmured Forquet. "From the wrong side. Perhaps if—"

"I knew *you* didn't have spades, partner," I broke in eagerly. "I had to draw an unusual inference, but you covered the point on page 19. I figured my spades were good enough to give us a play for it."

"Yes, I suppose so." Reese nodded thoughtfully. "I might remind you, however, that in my book your hand held K-10-x of spades—not K-x-x."

"Well, if we'd been bidding my way, you could have bid three spades asking *me* to bid three notrump with a spade stopper. That's just one of many useful conventions we could be using."

"I thought you didn't go in for artificialities," Reese rejoined drily. "Never mind. Next time I'll just bid four clubs."

"Well, I think it was unlucky," I said petulantly, pulling my cards out of the next board.

Reese started to say something but thought better of it. We

played out the remainder of the set in stony silence.

After the session Reese gave his scorecard to Konstam and scurried off to check on Schapiro. Konstam and Harrison-Gray disappeared to assess the damage, and I was left alone again in the auditorium. After about a half hour Konstam returned.

"How'd we do?" I asked.

"Lost 43 IMPs." He was ashen.

"You guys had a bad session." I tried to make this a statement rather than a query.

"I thought we played rather well," he grunted. "In fact, how in blazes—"

At that moment Harrison-Gray returned. "Come on," he said to Konstam. "We've got to talk to Reese about tonight."

I don't know what the British discussed during the next hour. Possibly there was some talk of pairing me with Konstam in an effort to steady him down. However, when the evening session began, I found Reese across the table again. He looked depressed.

"We'll get it back tonight," I assured him. Reese nodded grimly and picked up his cards.

North dealer
North-South vulnerable

```
                        North
                        ♠ Q J 5 2
                        ♡ 9 6 3
                        ◊ A 10 2
                        ♣ 10 7 2
        West                            East
        ♠ 6                             ♠ 9 7
        ♡ A K J 8 7 5                   ♡ Q 10 4
        ◊ 8 7 3                         ◊ J 6
        ♣ A J 3                         ♣ K Q 9 8 5 4
                        South
                        ♠ A K 10 8 4 3
                        ♡ 2
                        ◊ K Q 9 5 4
                        ♣ 6
```

Me	*Forquet*	*Reese*	*Garozzo*
South	West	North	East
—	—	pass	pass
1 ♠	2 ♡	2 ♠	3 ♡
(all pass)			

I overtook Reese's lead of the spade queen and tried to cash the ace. Forquet made twelve tricks.

"Well, we can't stop four," I observed, trying a little indirection.

"No, we can't," Reese agreed icily. "But don't you think you might have bid over three hearts?" And then his voice rose ever so slightly. "We can make *five* spades!"

"Well, of *course* I could have bid four spades directly," I explained patiently, "but I didn't want to have to contend with five hearts. You described the same situation on page 62 of your book. You said you would *admire* anyone who had the nerve to pass! How did I know it was going to get passed out?"

"If you recall," Reese gritted, "in my book I stressed the merits of *four diamonds.*"

"Well, I'm playing for admiration—not points," I whimpered.

Garozzo stifled a snicker and bid a spade.

```
                        North
                        ♠ J 5
                        ♡ A Q J 8 4
                        ◇ J 6 2
                        ♣ Q 9 4
        West                            East
        ♠ 6                             ♠ K 9 8 7 2
        ♡ 9 7 3 2                       ♡ 10
        ◇ Q 10 9                        ◇ A K 7 4
        ♣ K 10 7 5 3                    ♣ A J 6
                        South
                        ♠ A Q 10 4 3
                        ♡ K 6 5
                        ◇ 8 5 3
                        ♣ 8 2
```

Forquet	*Reese*	*Garozzo*	*Me*
West	North	East	South
—	—	1 ♠	pass
pass	double	pass	pass
1 NT	pass	2 ◇	double
(all pass)			

I led the eight of clubs. Garozzo took partner's queen and
finessed the nine of diamonds. Reese won and cashed the ace of
hearts. Garozzo ruffed the next round of hearts with the trump
ace and led a low diamond to the dummy. A third round of hearts
was ruffed with declarer's last diamond, after which Garozzo
played the jack of clubs to dummy's king. Then, with a Latin
shrug, he cashed the queen of diamonds. When that cleared up
the trumps there were three more clubs to cash, and two diamonds doubled made three.

Reese breathed a quiet oath and thrust his cards back in the
board. His hands were trembling slightly, and this struck me as
unusual in a player of Reese's stature. Why should the man be
nervous?

"I thought the hand would play badly for East," I explained.

"If you've got to double, can't you at least lead a heart?" demanded Reese. He sat with his hands clenched tightly on the table before him. His knuckles were white. I remember musing that even the greatest could become tense in a world championship match.

"I led a club," I replied, "because I expected to be ruffing behind declarer on the third round—just as you suggested on page 48 of your book. You were right, too, that my double would confuse declarer as to the disposition of the trumps. After all, you *did* make your jack. It was really very unlucky for us. If the diamonds had been 4-2 we'd—"

"I think we'd better get on with it," Forquet suggested.

"Quite," Reese agreed.

A few hands later an exciting situation arose:

```
                    North
                    ♠ A K 10 8 6 5
                    ♡ 3
                    ◊ 6 2
                    ♣ Q 10 4 3
    West                            East
    ♠ J 4 3                         ♠ Q 9 7 2
    ♡ K Q 10 8 6                    ♡ J 5 4
    ◊ Q 10 7                        ◊ 8
    ♣ A 5                           ♣ K 9 8 7 6
                    South
                    ♠ —
                    ♡ A 9 7 2
                    ◊ A K J 9 5 4 3
                    ♣ J 2
```

Forquet	Reese	Garozzo	Me
West	North	East	South
1 ♡	1 ♠	2 ♡	3 NT
pass	pass	double	redouble
(all pass)			

Forquet led the heart king, and continued with a low heart to the jack and ace. I cashed two rounds of diamonds and then gave up a diamond to West's queen. The hearts were cashed, then

```
                         North
                         ♠ A K 10 8 6 5
                         ♡ 3
                         ◊ 6 2
                         ♣ Q 10 4 3
        West                                East
        ♠ J 4 3                             ♠ Q 9 7 2
        ♡ K Q 10 8 6                        ♡ J 5 4
        ◊ Q 10 7                            ◊ 8
        ♣ A 5                               ♣ K 9 8 7 6
                         South
                         ♠ —
                         ♡ A 9 7 2
                         ◊ A K J 9 5 4 3
                         ♣ J 2
```

Forquet	Reese	Garozzo	Me
West	North	East	South
1 ♡	1 ♠	2 ♡	3 NT
pass	pass	double	redouble
(all pass)			

dummy was given the lead with a spade. Before I could build a club trick, the Italians had established a spade for themselves.

"Good grief," Reese muttered. "Did you have to redouble?"

"I was giving East the lash—just as you recommended on page 116," I retorted triumphantly. "After all, the diamonds might have run."

"If anything runs, it should have been me," Reese snorted. "I can make eight tricks in spades if I go about it right."

"Maybe so," I replied, "but—"

"—well-disciplined partners seldom take back into four spades after this sort of sequence," Reese recited sardonically. "I should know. I wrote it."

"1400?" asked Forquet politely.

Much later, after we had scored up the evening session, the afternoon decline had been most strongly confirmed. In fact, in the course of the day's play the British team had lost its 58-IMP edge—and 63 more. Reese called for the referee.

"The match is irretrievably lost," he declared. "But we British will play on. I do ask that we be permitted one change in our team. There's a code clerk at the British embassy who plays a fairish game."

"Who's going out?" I broke in anxiously. "You gonna put this guy in for Konstam?"

Reese nodded. "We'll see," he muttered inscrutably.

I found Reese at lunch the next day talking earnestly with a drab little chap who looked every inch a reincarnation of one of that vast group of colonial functionaries who once virtually administered the earth. I broke in—rudely perhaps—to ask about the line-up. Reese was surprisingly amiable.

"I'm going to try it today with Farthingale. Both sessions. Konstam and Harrison-Gray in the closed room."

"Oh." I reflected on the firmness with which Reese had articulated *both sessions*. "Then I guess that's it for me?"

Reese nodded and looked out the window at some children who were throwing rocks at a statue of George Washington. Then the two of them got up and started towards the door. I followed them out.

"Well, I enjoyed it," I ventured feebly. "Sorry we didn't have better luck."

"Quite." Reese was paying his bill.

"Actually, I thought we did well on most of the hands," I continued. "If our partners had just—"

Reese cut me off with a noncommittal grunt. "Now really, old chap, Bruce and I must get to our places. Remember what happened yesterday." He shivered slightly I thought, although it was quite warm. They started off together. I stood there momentarily, uncertain, then scurried after them.

"Wait," I panted. "Next time I'm in London—we'll have a game, won't we?"

Reese smiled patiently. "Of course, old boy." But he had turned away and was talking intently to the clerk. "Now, in the Little Major, if I open—"

I sprinted after them again. "Wait! *I'll* play the Little Major if *that's* what you want. And Acol two-bids, and transfers, and—" I seized Reese—almost angrily it seemed—and we struggled for a moment on the street. Then that swine Farthingale pinioned my arms, and two policemen were kicking me, and I was falling . . . .

I awakened on the floor—partially enshrouded in a blanket—
with my wife peering angrily over the precipice above.

"For Pete's sake," she ranted. "What's *wrong* with you?"

I lay there in a sort of daze for a full five seconds. "I've just
been kicked off the British World Championship Team." I pulled
myself back into bed. "I'll tell you all about it tomorrow morning."

The Pain Factor
by Matthew Granovetter

ALERT! THIS IS NOT an article about any of the more intriguing aspects of an upside-down coup. Nor shall you read of how to reach a 4-3 grand-slam fit with artificial relays, denial cue bids, and a few simple transfers. In fact, if you learn anything of value, it will be how to prepare and cushion yourself for the avalanche to come: defeat. For some readers, my own personal and painful reminiscences might be too much to bear; and those dear friends should skip on to less realistic items.

Pain! See, I told you this would not be easy. *Aagghh!* The pain is unbearable; but comprehensible. Henceforth we shall identify it as "The Pain Factor."

Supposition: You have entered the tournament with the goal of winning. You have lost the tournament.

Theorem 1: The Pain Factor is inversely proportional to your final standing in the tournament.

Theorem 2: The Pain Factor is inversely proportional to the difference between your score and the winning score.

In other words, it's better to be 100th than second. It's better to lose by nine boards than by half a matchpoint.

The Pain Factor can be divided into 4 general areas of torture:
(1) Initial shock and hysteria;
(2) The green blah;
(3) Self-guilt;
(4) Return to the scene of the crime.

We will examine exhibits taken from real life.

Atlanta, Spring 1971. The two-day Swiss. My team: Kathy Wei, Benito Garozzo, Jim Becker, me. Near the end. Dummy has K-10-9-x-x in a side suit; I, declarer, hold A-x. I have one trump in my hand to ruff out this suit. Cannot lose a trick. I call low from dummy. L.O.L. plays the jack. I win the ace and lead back to dummy's king, everyone following low. I call the ten. Low. What now? I discard . . . *queen!* A twinge of pain shoots through me. We lose the tournament. "How did you go down in this contract?" asks Benito. Why does he ask this? Doesn't he know I am in pain? "The suit divided 3-3." Will there always be this pain?

We are in St. Louis, 1972. We have just completed the last 18 deals of a Vanderbilt knock-out match. Going into the last quarter our team was +69 IMPs. Needless to say, Ronnie Rubin and I have just had a poor set. Yet there is this slight recollection of our half-time dinner festivities. Had it been so long ago? I remember the champagne Sam Stayman had bought for the team. So what if we now have one bad set of results? Can we really weigh this poor quarter against three magnificent sets?

How poor were these 18 results? Well, Bud Reinhold bid a slam on two finesses; that was bad for us. They did make a funny-looking three notrump; not so hot. But against that had we not made a game when the defenders crashed their ace and king of trumps? Also, that hand where we stayed out of slam, needing to lose no tricks with ace-king-jack-nine-fifth opposite three small. I had cleverly cashed the ace and king. Queen-ten-fourth were onside. Probably a pickup for us. Gee, why am I concerned?

We are waiting for our teammates to compare scores. Mr. Stayman has gone upstairs to rest for tomorrow's match. Mr. Mitchell has taken his position in the coffee shop. Oh, there they come from the Closed Room where they played against Dr. Katz and Mr. Cohen (whoever they are). "How'd you do?" chirps a cheery me. "Terrible, terrible, worst game we ever had," quoth they. "Then we're in trouble," says Ronnie.

Are you kidding? +69? I think this, but I am afraid to say it out loud. We begin to add (subtract) the IMPs. "Minus 11 . . . minus 13 . . . minus . . ." The air is getting thick. Yet wait, wait, I remember our last board. Our opponents went down in a hopeless 4-3 slam; yes, yes, I remember! ". . . minus 6. . . minus 5. . . what contract were you in? . . ." Why am I so hot? I take a peek at board 72, the last board. We *do* win 11 imps! Ronnie is keeping a running total. "Minus 53. . . minus 61. . . minus 74. . . minus 83. . ." What! Only one more board to go. . .add. . .subtract. . .subtract. . . I hear a fantastic shrill sound, a victory shriek from a short distance away. Arms are flying. "We lost," is mumbled near me. Cannot inhale. Am going to faint. Move. Move quickly. Wait. Not towards the shrill shriek. Away. The service elevator. Quickly. *Who am I? Where am I?*

How often I still awake in the middle of the night to the sound of that victory shriek!

There were a number of things to be learned from my St. Louis experience. One, finesse the nine with ace-king-jack-nine-fifth. Two, always keep a current track of the IMP score (e.g., +3, +12, +21, +19) rather than the score for each hand (+3, +9, +9, -2), so that at the end you will not have to add and subtract to realize your final result. This method of scoring (now known as the "anti-shriek method") enables you to learn the result of the match before your opponents, thereby giving you sufficient time to cover your ears. Three, and most important, never enter the playing quarters the day after you have lost.

Miami, Summer 1975. "Oh, you're still playing bridge? I'd have given up by now if I were . . . ." I scoffed at such comments. After all, was I not still alive and well after being the victim of three similar catastrophes in three consecutive years? I remember: fleeing from Vancouver in the wee hours of the morning, rushing out of the N.Y. Americana into a mad traffic jam to calm myself after losing 97 IMPs, and finally, standing around in a stunned silence accepting my fate from the bridge gods after losing the Grand Nationals in Miami. Was I finally becoming immune? I went upstairs to my room and faced my packed bags. (Al Roth: "Always keep your bags packed.") But, alas, the Spingold was still to come. I went to the phone. "I'd like an early reservation to New York." I was learning.

It was during this event, as my team steam-rolled along, devastating the opposition, that I had a brief encounter with John Swanson. He was in the lobby, bags in hand, ready to depart. "Oh well, you can't win 'em all." I thought, had he won *any?* Yes, yes, a long time ago. "You don't look so well, John. Have you by any chance been near the playing quarters?" He did not have to answer. It was a clear case of the "Green Blah." This cursed disease will conquer any fool who enters the playing room the day after his demise. The strongest attack of Green Blah comes directly from the table occupied by your opponents from the previous day. They are occupying what would have been *your* seats. Do not look in that direction. There is no cure for the Green Blah. It numbs you, consumes you with grief, stifles your physical movements. Most Green Blah victims are not heard from for many months, sometimes years.

Round-of-8, Miami Spingold. Rapee vs. Guiver. Three-quarter mark: Rapee +50. Mr. Rapee retires to his room to rest for tomorrow's match. Mr. Grieve takes his position in the bar. I do not take this lightly. Final instructions to my anchor pair in the Closed Room, Lipsitz and Parker: "Remember fellas, +50 is no laughing matter. Be careful." They laugh.

Nothing bad happens to Jimmy Cayne and me on our first eight boards. I relax. The ninth hand: My opponent misplays a four-heart contract. Having forgotten to draw trumps with ace-king-ten-fourth opposite queen-fourth, he gives us the chance for a trump promotion. But he ruffs with the queen and finesses my jack-third to score his contract the hard way. No swing, think I, but a bad sign. We miss a slam. A worse sign. And now the holocaust. I hold: ♠ x ♡ A K x x x ◊ A K x x x x x ♣ —.

Better bid this one right. "One diamond." "Pass." "Two notrump," Jimmy says. "Pass." What now? It's very late and we're both tired. Wonder what they did with this hand in the other room. Leap to seven diamonds? That's what *I* would do minus 50 IMPs. If I bid Gerber, he'll surely show one ace; forget that. C'mon bid seven diamonds like a man. Wait. Must bid intelligently. Owe it to the team. Maybe partner can cue-bid spades.

"Three hearts." "Pass." "Three spades." "Pass." Great! Now seven diamonds. Wait. . .forgot. . .we discussed cue bids below three notrump; they may be concentrated strength rather than the ace. What now? Cannot bid four hearts; may get passed. Cannot bid four diamonds, same thing. *Got it!* I'll bid four *clubs.* He'll probably bid four diamonds. I'll come back with five clubs. He'll return to five diamonds and I'll continue with five hearts. This will force a spade cue bid if he has the ace; then I can bid seven diamonds. Good thinking.

"Four clubs." "Pass." "Four diamonds." "Pass." Perfect! Just as anticipated. On to the next round: "Five clubs." "Pass." Jimmy is thinking, thinking. Oh my God, what is he thinking of? Didn't I deny clubs with my three heart call? C'mon Jimmy, bid. Bid! I don't believe this. *Bid!!*

"Pass," Jimmy says! (Feels like I've just been hit with a sledgehammer.)

We come out. Our teammates come out. "How'd you do?" I cough. "How did *you* do?" retort they. (By far, this is the worst answer one can receive.)

Lose 60 imps. Lose the match. Exit Jimmy Cayne from bridge for two years. Exit me with my hands over my ears.

Ah yes, the pain was bad; but I was a big boy. I had seen it all before. I am therefore going to conquer this feeling. The hell with bridge; I go dancing. Yes! Dancing! I will drown my sorrows in wine and music. Off I go. . .must forget. . .forget. Round and round I go. Forget. Must forget. . . . "Lucy in the sky-y with *diamonds.* . . ." Aagghh! Round and round. . .please forget... please. . . . "For diamonds are a girl's best friend. . . ." For diamonds. Oh no. *Four diamonds!* Why didn't I jump to four diamonds over two notrump? It's *my* fault. *My* fault! (Round and round, up and down. . .and down. . .and down. . . .)

Years later.

"I'm coming out of retirement."

"That's brave, Jimmy. What event?"

"The Reisinger Board-a-Match team event. It's got everything going for it. The directors do the adding of the score; you can't get knocked out; and the tournament is over for everyone at the same time (no Green Blah)."

In November of 1977 I returned to the scene of the crime. Atlanta. I remember it well. I was young and foolish then. Today I am ready. Bring on the pain. Bring on defeat. I am ready.

Last day of the tournament. My team is leading in the Reisinger. We have completed over a hundred deals. They are gone, forgotten. There is one round to be played and we are still leading. Jimmy's team is close behind. Hmmm. This could be painful for somebody (think I). Bridge-wise, I am rolling. All my decisions have been double-dummy. I just balanced with two notrump over a weak two spade bid with 10-x-x of spades; partner held Q-x-x. I'm rolling. Here come Kyle Larsen and Mike Lawrence, Jimmy's teammates. They had been leading at the end of the afternoon despite losing all three boards to us.

Three deals to play. Hand 1: We reach four spades. I hold A-10-9-8-x of spades, dummy has the singleton king. Somehow I trump four cards in my hand to land the contract. I'm rolling. Hand 2: They squirm their way to four hearts. I'm rolling, so I double. They don't redouble. They make five. Hand 3: nondescript. I ain't rolling anymore. The session is over.

Jimmy wins! More important, we lose. Most important, we are second by only .27 of a board. Since a team must win by .25, we have actually lost this event by .02 of a board. Had I not doubled four hearts we would have won easily. I am not in pain; I have transcended pain. I rise from the table. Someone in the distance calls out, "Is the carry-over accurate?" An angel is speaking. Did the directors make an error in the carry-over? I turn my head and spot Jimmy. Oh, what the hell! Am I not better insulated for the pain than he is? In fact, there could be more pain for me to see *him* in pain that to be in pain myself! I think of a new theorem.

Theorem 3: Friendship overrides the Pain Factor. All these years, and now I have found the answer. Ahh, how sweet it is. Tranquility. Contentment. "Why did you double four hearts?" some devil asks.

"Check those carry-over figures!!" I scream.

VII
Back on the Road

Safari Bridge

A COUPLE OF MONTHS AGO my girlfriend, Judy, who works for American Airlines, asked me if I would like to go on a safari. I thought she was kidding. Until then I was happy watching Lorne Green on the tube telling me about those wild animals.

Of course we went. But we decided to do it up right and visit some friends as well.

The trip started in London, where we stayed at the flat (notice how I pick up the lingo) of my good friend and British internationalist, Robert Sheehan. In fact, Robert is such a good friend that he moved out of his own place into a friend's flat during our stay.

I wouldn't say he was happy to see us leave, but on the last morning of our stay he phoned and asked me to remove some chicken from the freezer—one piece.

The highlight of the stay in London was dinner with my good friend Jonathan Cansino, who seems to be doing quite well after some serious brain surgery. Jonathan, by the way, before the surgery was clearly one of the best bridge players in the world. I know, I played with him quite a bit.

I might as well throw in my two favorite Cansino stories here. The first takes place in Denver where we were playing in the Open Pairs in an extremely noisy room.

After Jonathan opened four spades, holding eight spades to the K-Q-J-10, the opponents wound up in five hearts, doubled by me, only Jonathan thought that the final contract was five notrump doubled.

He led the king of spades and dummy won the singleton ace of spades (declarer and I each had a small doubleton). At trick two I got the lead and was pondering what to do. I finally decided to force the dummy with a spade. I played my spade. At this point, Jonathan, who was still defending five notrump doubled, said, "what took you so bloody long?"

Although declarer ruffed in dummy, Jonathan proceeded to "run" his spades, revoking five times before we sorted out what happened. Oh well, we couldn't beat five hearts doubled anyway.

Over the years Jonathan played quite successfully with Robert Sheehan, one of Great Britain's finest players. It so happened that after one particularly disastrous session they weren't speaking to each other at all. Finally, Sheehan approached Jonathan with a small piece of blank paper and said, "Here, Jonathan, write down all you know about bridge."

Jonathan replied, "Well, it's a bigger piece of paper than I would have given you."

The next leg of the trip was Nairobi, Kenya, for a seven day safari. By the way, safaris these days are limited to hunting with cameras. You don't shoot them and they don't eat you. It all works out very nicely.

From Nairobi we went to Bella Roma via Athens because A'litalia was on one of its 24 hour strikes that lasted 13 days. Once at the hotel, I decided to call Giorgio Belladonna because: (1) I knew he owned a bridge club and (2) he has beaten me twice in the World Championships. So we must be good friends.

Wonder of wonders, he was home and invited Judy and me to dinner at his club the following night when they had their big team game.

Now for a word about the players in the team game. Benito Garozzo and Lea du Pont had just left Turin and were moving into Giorgio's club. They, along with Georgio and me, were to play against an Italian team which was preparing for a play-off to determine Italy's representative in the European Championships a few months later.

I was to play the first half with Giorgio. Benito and Lea would play their special Precision system that only two people in the world are capable of remembering—and they haven't found those people yet.

The way Giorgio tells it, when he plays this system with Benito and he puts his dummy down, Benito asks Lea, who is always kibitzing, to check in the "book" to see whether or not Giorgio has bid properly!

Giorgio and I decided to play "naturale," with Giorgio looking to the heavens after making this concession.

Things were going along fairly well when I picked up vulnerable vs. not: ♠ Q ♡ A K ◇ A K J 10 6 5 ♣ 7 5 3 2.

I was sitting South, against a pair using the Roman Club, and the bidding went:

West	North	East	South (Me)
1 NT	pass	2 ♡	3 ◇
pass	pass	3 ♠	?

As usual, I didn't know what to do, so I tried three notrump. It went pass on my left and Giorgio bid four clubs. Now I didn't know whether he thought I had clubs or whether he had clubs. Wonderful. I decided to raise to five clubs. This was greeted by a rather vicious "contro" (we were bidding in English until then) on my left and everyone passed.

The lead was made and I asked Giorgio if I could see his hand. This is what I saw: ♠ A 6 4 2 ♡ 9 7 3 ◇ 3 2 ♣ 9 8 6 4.

We were off 150 honors in clubs for openers. No matter how the clubs were divided I knew I would not be invited back for another dinner (I was).

Furthermore, if clubs were four-one I might not have enough lira to get out of the club, never mind the country.

Fortunately, clubs were three-two and Giorgio managed to get out for down one, allowing his partner to breathe once again.

Nevertheless, our team was down 20 IMPs at the half, so we decided to switch partnerships. This time I played with Lea, with no kibitzers, and Giorgio played with Benito, with 80 kibitzers.

I say this because there were so few witnesses to my finest hour. After a sequence that I would rather not admit, I arrived at a contract of three diamonds doubled with the following cards:

North (Lea)
♠ A 8 6 5 4
♡ 2
◊ A 2
♣ A K J 9 7

West
♠ K J 9 2
♡ A 3
◊ K J 9 6 5
♣ Q 5

East
♠ Q 10 3
♡ K Q 10 9 8 5
◊ 7
♣ 10 6 4

South (Me)
♠ 7
♡ J 7 6 4
◊ Q 10 8 4 3
♣ 8 3 2

The ace of hearts was led and I ruffed the heart continuation. I played the ace and ruffed a spade, crossed to a club and ruffed another spade. Back to a club followed by another spade ruff, East discarding a club.

At this point West is down to a trump flush and I have seven tricks. I ruffed a heart with the ace of diamonds, West under-ruffing, and led a club. East ruffed, but I discarded. West under-ruffed but had to ruff East's heart play and concede a ninth trick to my queen of diamonds.

After a lovely set we discovered we had picked up 19 IMPs. As losers do, we rechecked the score a few dozen times, but finally I had to admit that I had lost a team match with Garozzo and Belladonna as teammates!

There were still a few extra days before the Nationals, so we went to New York looking for more friends to stay with. (It was sure nice to have so many friends before this trip, because now we don't have any.)

I tried calling one of my friends. You may have heard of her. Teri Garr. In fact, we call her Teri Garr, Superstar. She has appeared in "Tootsie" and many other hit movies. I knew her before she became so famous because she lived in an apartment adjoining mine for about five years. As a matter of fact, I even took her out after she first moved in. When I took her home and wanted to kiss her goodnight, she said, "Take it easy buddy, I'm on a year's lease."

Rumor has it that she moved out to get away from me. But it didn't work. I tracked her down, and we wound up staying in her apartment in Greenwich Village.

Soon it was time to travel on to the Nationals in Norfolk, Virginia. I was to play with John Mohan. The last time I played with John we played four-card majors, and our results left a little to be desired.

This time I was greeted with "Five-card majors in first and second, Drury, forcing notrump, two over one game force, Astro, Flannery, Weak Twos, 15-17 notrump, Forcing Stayman and Jacoby. The rest of the card is yours." Thanks John. We did better, but not quite good enough. We lost in the quarterfinals to the Stayman team.

At last I was able to return to my beloved Venice Beach in Los Angeles. It had been a great trip, but, after all, there's no place like home.

Comparing scores with Giorgio during a practice match in Geneva.

Judy feeding me at Venice Beach.

The Coach

JUST IN CASE you don't know it, I have been appointed coach of the North American Team which will compete in the World Championship next May in Miami Beach.

The coach is supposed to be completely fluent with all of the systems that the Italians, French, etc. will be playing. Therefore, my first assignment as coach was to have two of the members of the team, Sammy Kehela, and Edgar Kaplan teach me the Roman and the Neopolitan Club. After all, Edgar has written a book on the subject and Sammy knows both systems as well as the Colonial Acol system that he plays with Eric Murray. Besides, I'm not proud as long as nobody knows that they are teaching me. (Shhh. . .)

Another one of my duties is to observe the members of the team in action during practice matches and perhaps offer a helpful word or two. The fact that I am younger than any of the players other than Kehela is not supposed to matter. After all, I am the coach.

Actually, I have played against all of the members of this year's team in the Trials and I have a few minor suggestions which I will make to them when I see them. Oh, I forgot to mention that two of the players live in Canada, three in New York and one in Philadelphia. It is considered in the best interests of the team if the coach lives as far away as possible from the team members. Nevertheless, I will be heard! These are my preliminary minor suggestions:

To Roth and Root: Give up five-card majors and the strong notrump and adopt the weak notrump with four-card majors. I offer the following hand as proof positive that the weak notrump and four-card majors are best:

Opener	Responder
♠ K Q 7 6	♠ 5 3
♡ A Q 6 5	♡ J 8 3 2
◇ Q 10 6	◇ A K J 5
♣ A 7	♣ 10 6 5

Playing the way Roth and Root play the bidding might be:

Opener	Responder
1 NT	2 ♣
2 ♡	4 ♡

This would make exactly four and probably tie the board against the Italians. Now look at the sequence that they can never have without playing the weak notrump.

Opener	Responder
1 ♠	1 NT
2 NT	3 NT

The opener cannot open one notrump (perish the thought) and would never be caught dead opening a short minor. Therefore, the correct opening bid is one spade. Responder must bid one notrump, and the opener is too strong to bid two hearts and too weak to bid three hearts, so must content himself with two notrump. Responder is maximum and goes to game, which is defeated two tricks with a club lead. But look how smoothly the auction flows!

To Murray and Kehela, To Kehela and Murray: (There's no jealousy in this partnership but if you use one name before the other you are liable to the most exquisite forms of torture from the offended party.) Stop opening so light, and being so aggressive. You are making **me** nervous. Why, I saw Murray open the following dog, vulnerable: ♠ A J 4 3 2 ♡ 2 ◊ A 5 4 3 2 ♣ 3 2.

No doubt impressed with his spot cards, he opened one spade. Had he passed, his left hand opponent would have opened one spade and his right hand opponent would have bid two clubs. On his left would have come two hearts and on his right three hearts and on his left four hearts. This could have been defeated one trick. But no, Murray had to open with that piece of dogmeat. This was the entire deal:

```
                     North (Kehela)
                     ♠ 5
                     ♡ A 7 5
                     ◊ Q 10 9 8 7 6
                     ♣ A 7 6
  West                                East
  ♠ K Q 10 8 7                        ♠ 9 6
  ♡ K J 9 8 6                         ♡ Q 10 4 3
  ◊ J                                 ◊ K
  ♣ 10 5                              ♣ K Q J 9 8 4
                     South (Murray)
                     ♠ A J 4 3 2
                     ♡ 2
                     ◊ A 5 4 3 2
                     ♣ 3 2
```

This was the bidding:

Murray		*Kehela*	
South	West	North	East
1 ♠	2 ♡	3 ◊	4 ♡
5 ◊	5 ♡	6 ◊	double
(all pass)			

Opening lead: ♣ King (making just six)

To Kaplan and Kay: Give up leading ace from ace-king fifth against notrump. Lead fourth best from those suits! Why, here is a hand in point from the qualifying round of the Trials. Edgar Kaplan held this hand: ♠ Q 9 3 ♡ A K 8 5 3 ◊ Q 10 6 ♣ 5 4.

The bidding went one notrump (weak, naturally) on his right. He passed. (Murray probably would have overcalled.) It went three notrump on his left. Now, do you know what Edgar Kaplan led from this hand? Believe it or not, the ace of hearts! Imagine, the ace of hearts with no sure entry. This was the deal:

                          North
                          ♠ K J 4
                          ♡ 7 4 2
                          ◊ K 2
                          ♣ A Q J 10 2
    West (Edgar)   East (Norman)
    ♠ Q 9 3   ♠ 10 8 6 5
    ♡ A K 8 5 3   ♡ J 9 6
    ◊ Q 10 6   ◊ 9 7 5 3
    ♣ 5 4   ♣ 9 8
                          South
                          ♠ A 7 2
                          ♡ Q 10
                          ◊ A J 8 4
                          ♣ K 7 6 3

So it happened to work this time. So what? So they took the first five heart tricks. So Norman Kay unblocked with the nine and then the jack. So I was the only player in the Trials not to make three notrump. So what? I'm not bitter. . . . I have just one more comment to make—Fellows, please! Stop playing so well or I'll never make the team as a player, only a coach.

The Vacation

SOMETHING NEW and wonderful has been added to the bridge scene—Club Med hosted a one week bridge festival in Guadaloupe.

For a package price of $900.00 (air fare included from Miami or New York) you can have the time of your life and play bridge every day from four to eight in the evening.

Of course you have to like the sun, water sports, tennis, golf, a beautiful beach, great food and professional entertainment each night after dinner. If not, this is not the place for you.

The kickoff for this tournament was a Calcutta run by Billy Eisenberg and Mike Moss. Mike doubled as the auctioneer. Twenty-two pairs were auctioned off, including one which was sure to self-destruct: Alvin Roth and Amos Kaminski.

The year before I had played with Amos in the Blue Ribbon Pairs and he is quite a character. A typically aggressive Israeli with an advanced sense of humor, he was not above asking any opponent who had erred against us, "And from which village did you qualify?"

However, playing with Roth is something else. Not a word was heard from Amos. He was too busy listening. Before the beginning of the third session I asked Amos if they had self-destructed yet. He said no, but he also said he would be playing better bridge with his nine-year-old son who doesn't know how to play. He said he was now conducting sequences which would lead to the least number of insults after the bidding was over.

The tone of the auction was set when Mike Moss, playing with Marvin Rosenblatt, was auctioning himself off. His ex, Gail, made a substantial bid and Mike said, "It won't work, you can't have me back, and don't expect to use the alimony to pay." Gail, of course, takes all this in stride.

Playing with Bobby Goldman against Gail and Ahmed Hussein, the following bidding sequence developed when they held these cards:

West (Ahmed)	East (Gail)
♠ 2	♠ Q J 3
♡ A Q J 3	♡ 4
◇ A 10	◇ Q 9 8 7 6
♣ A J 10 9 8 7	♣ 6 4 3 2
1 ♣	1 ◇
1 ♡	2 ♣
4 ♠ !	5 ♣
pass	

After everyone passed, I asked Gail about that four spade bid. She said it was a splinter jump. I asked her what three spades would have meant. She said that would also be a splinter. Silence descended upon the table. Finally, she added, "this was a dramatic splinter."

Midway through the Open Pairs Bobby decided he wanted to bid in French. Oh no, I thought, shades of Billy. Billy used to try to bid in French. It took me four years to discover that when he bid "sans atout" (no trump) he had stoppers in all four suits, and when he bid "sans atoit," he didn't.

Bobby, a little more organized, decided to create his own phonetic transliteration for the suits and numbers. Coeur (hearts) became "cur;" carreaux (diamonds) became "carow;" piques (spades) became "peak;" sept (seven) became "set," etc.

After a while, if the opponents understood his French he thought he was making the right bid! Finally, in a gesture of total arrogance he threw away his phonetic sheet and decided to have a go on his own.

Everything was going just fine until he opened "un cur" (one heart), was raised to two curs and wanted to make a game try in diamonds. Forgetting the word for diamonds, but barely remembering the one for clubs, he emerged with "twa trefla." This was supposed to be "trois trefles" (three clubs), but to me it sounded like it rhymed with "kreplach."

Anyway, we wound up in three hearts. Is it any wonder that the opponents did not find the right defense?

The tournament ended with a glorious awards ceremony. However, just before the professional entertainment they herded Mike Moss, Marvin Rosenblatt, Bobby, Billy and myself backstage and told us to put on tutus!

They also gave us stuffing up top, wigs, painted our faces, including blackening our teeth, and gave us a pair of snorkel flippers. This was to be our outfit for the opening number, "Swan Lake."

Billy's wife, Dominique, told us to pretend we were birds when the music started, and when it finally slowed down to put our arms over our heads and turn around slowly.

Don't ask. The song lasted three minutes but it seemed as if we were out there an hour. When the music ended, mercifully, we went backstage to thunderous non-applause.

At this time the real performers went on stage and the music for the can-can started. "Sure," said Marvin Rosenblatt, "now that we're through they play the easy stuff."

In the interest of honest reporting, it must be mentioned that there was a nudie beach at this Club Med village. Strangely, this turned out to be a very popular walk for the bridge players.

In fact, I mentioned to Marvin that I had taken the walk so many times I was beginning to know the people by name.

"And without even looking at their faces," he added.

Club Med, Guadaloupe, 1978. Left to right: Judy, me,
Elyakim Shaufel, Bobby Goldman, Diana Gordon, David Birman.

The year before with one of my favorite partners, Don Krauss
—at the Maccabiah Games in Israel.

The Paris-Israel Connection

As LONG AS they keep inviting us, we'll keep going. This time Billy Eisenberg and I were invited to take part in two money tournaments. The first was in Paris—the famous Del Duca tournament, beautifully organized by the late Dr. Pierre Jais, held June 6 and 7. The second was in Israel, in Caesarea to be exact, from June 8-13.

We arrived in Paris a few days early to beat the jet lag. It didn't help. After a strong first session, we had about an average game the second session, so even though they paid down 50 places, our names were nowhere to be seen on that list.

We did have our moments, however, some good and some bad. Might as well get the horror story out of the way. Of course, you have to understand when you play in a European tournament, you expect to get at least one awful result because either you or your partner will mistake one honor card for another due to a lack of familiarity with the French playing cards.

This time it was Billy. Of course, I should have been prepared because the last time we played in Europe he got mad at me for not covering dummy's queen with my jack.

This time he was West and I was East and these were our cards:

West (Billy)	East (Me)
(blind as a bat)	*(helpless victim)*
♠ Q J 10 8 7	♠ A
♡ A J 10 8 3 2	♡ Q 5
◊ J 4	◊ Q 10
♣ —	♣ A K Q J 8 7 4 3

With both sides vulnerable, Billy thought he had the spade king-queen and decided to open the hand with one spade.

I tried a jump to three clubs which showed one of three types of hands: (1) a long solid-like club suit; (2) a notrump type hand with a five or six card club suit; (3) a spade fit.

In any case, we play that a new suit by the opener now shows two of the top three honors with no reference to length. So what could poor Billy do?

He decided to rebid three spades. I bid four clubs, and he persisted with four spades. Do you like this system?

Breaking all Blackwood rules, I tried four notrump. When Billy responded five diamonds, I launched straight away into six notrump. The lady on lead tried the diamond ace from A-x-x. Six diamond tricks later, I was down five, vulnerable.

Even though we didn't scratch in Paris, we could hardly call it a bad trip. Not only was the weather perfect, but Billy and I were wined and dined. A word to the wise: Ami Louis, 123 rue de Bois Vert. If I were you, I wouldn't turn down an invitation to L'Orangerie either.

Billy and I were invited to L'Orangerie by the Brazilian bridge whiz, Gabriel Chagas. Gabriel now represents a Brazilian soybean company that does much of its business in France. As Gabriel is very personable and speaks 11 languages fluently, he frequently finds himself in Paris. He even has a chauffeur at his disposal!

His chauffeur is so elegant that Gabriel sometimes finds himself calling the chauffeur "Sir."

At dinner, he told us of his pre-soybean gambling days. Once he was involved in a high-stakes poker game when his wife called. This was strictly forbidden. She was not supposed to call him during this game.

As it turned out, he was losing heavily, and the call for him to bring home some milk for the baby did not go over very well with him. In fact, he lost a fortune that night.

When he came home to his wife (seething), he told her that he had some good news and some bad news for her. "The good news is that I brought home the milk; the bad news is that I have just lost our apartment." It was true! But his friends bailed him out. Now, of course, he has no more financial worries.

The second leg of our trip was a brand-new tournament organized by a non-bridge player who is interested in promoting events of this kind in Israel. His name is Armand Cohen. He is a dentist who lives in Paris but travels frequently to Israel and even has a home in Caesarea, a small village-like place on the Mediterranean in the northern part of Israel.

Armand has more enthusiasm in his little finger than most of us can conjure up in a lifetime. What a week he showed us in Caesarea! But I am getting a bit ahead of myself.

The day we were to leave Paris I glanced at my precious International Herald Tribune, lifeline to my other world, where my beloved Lakers were playing for the NBA championship (without me), and Holmes and Cooney were fighting for the heavyweight title without waiting for me to get back. Silent death.

The headlines were a bit disturbing that day. "Israel attacks Lebanon—full-scale war in progress." This is where I was going?

As a safety play, I called the State Department. Maybe there was a misprint in the paper. No, no misprint. In fact, they said don't go, it is dangerous there.

"Billy," I said, "there is a war going on—why should we go? We don't need the master points."

I knew I was talking to the wrong person. "Not to worry," Billy said. "Everything will be O.K."

Armand was already in Israel, so I called his wife. She said Armand had just called and told her it was safe. I called the two French players who were also invited, Paul Chemla and Christian Mari. Their response was very reassuring: "If we die, we die."

So of course, we went. The cab driver, a friend of Armand, told us that Caesarea was about 90 minutes by cab from the fighting. We thanked him for that little tidbit of information, at the same time telling him we weren't interested in getting any closer.

Well, here we were at the Dan Caesarea, a truly beautiful hotel, once used as a Club Med facility and guess what—not too many people showed up. Everybody was fighting in the war. In Israel, everyone fights.

Have you ever seen the bumper sticker that says: "What if they gave a war and nobody came?" In Israel they should have one that reads "What if they gave a bridge tournament and everyone went to war?"

As we arrived one day after the three-session pair game was in progress, the director, Israel Erdenbaum, said he would average our two remaining scores and use that as a barometer for our missing session.

The good news is that we won the tournament by a mile; the bad news is that they cancelled the prize money because so few people showed up. Oh well, they are going to have this tournament next year, and without a war it should be something else.

There were a few language problems. Armand, Paul, and Christian all speak English rather well but prefer, of course, to speak French. Billy's French is such that they were forced to speak English. Some strange sentence structures were to be heard. Once Billy was playing tennis against Christian and Billy double-faulted. Christian said, "I am very sorry." Billy answered, in French, "I am worse sorry." On another occasion, "Do you have money on you?" "Yes, I have many money." And, "Please open more the window." By the way, this is the way we were speaking, not the French!

What a trip!

The Flight Home

I COULD NEVER REMEMBER being quite so tired. The night before our team had just blown a two-board lead going into the final session of the Reisinger Board-a-Match Teams and finished sixth out of ten.

Now here it was early the next morning, the end of a long Thanksgiving weekend, and American Airlines was offering first $300.00 then $500.00 and finally $1,000.00 in vouchers to anyone who would give up his seat and take the next flight out four hours later. Only one of our group took the deal. We all wanted to go home.

I was sitting on the aisle with a vacant window seat to my left, wondering how I was going to kill four-plus hours, when Pam Wittes approached. She told me she had exchanged her seat with a couple to accommodate them, and could she sit by the window. Of course.

Pam Wittes, in case you don't know, won the World Mixed Pairs Championship in partnership with her husband Jon in Miami Beach several years ago. Coincidentally, she and Jon had just been interviewed in "Bridge Today" and I had read the interview with interest.

The gist of the article was how they dealt with each other's bridge blunders at the table. Judging from what I read, Pam had a much better "table temperament" than Jon, but Jon was working

on improving that aspect of his game. In fact, the article said that
Pam never said word one to Jon during the game. If something
went wrong she talked to him about it at home later, construc-
tively. What a woman!

Well, there we were with four hours to kill and I couldn't
sleep. I decided to do a crossword puzzle. It was such an easy one
that I didn't have to ask Pam for assistance even though I thought
she was aching to have a go at it.

Finally, I decided to ask her if she wanted to do a bid-em-up
from an Italian magazine. "Sure." I handed her a list of eight hands
and explained to her that an "R" meant a king, a "D" a queen, and
an "F" a jack. She immediately made all the corrections in pen.
We were ready to bid.

On the first hand we arrived at the top spot. We're on a roll, I
thought.

This was my second hand: ♠ K 8 5 3 ♡ A 3 ◇ A 8 4 ♣ 6 5 3 2.
Our bidding started like this:

Pam	Me
1 ◇	1 ♠
2 ◇	?

It seemed to me my choices were three diamonds, two
notrump or three notrump. Wanting to show Pam I was no sissy, I
jumped to three notrump on the strength of my fitting ace of
diamonds. Pam passed.

Hand two:

Pam	Me
♠ A 2	♠ K 8 5 3
♡ K Q 4 2	♡ A 3
◇ Q J 10 7 3 2	◇ A 8 4
♣ 4	♣ 6 5 3 2

Had I rebid either two notrump or three diamonds we would
have ended up in the proper contract of five diamonds. Pam
looked at my hand and noticed my clubs. "Dummy," she said, "we
can make five diamonds."

I apologized and we moved on. I survived hands three and four, but then there was hand five. I picked up:

♠ J 10 9 ♡ A 6 ◇ K J ♣ A K 9 7 5 2.

I opened one notrump. Pam responded two diamonds, transfer, and I rebid two hearts. Pam continued with three diamonds showing a forcing-to-game hand with hearts and diamonds. Fearing three notrump because of the spades, and not wanting to bid four clubs, which I thought would sound like a cue bid, I meekly bid three hearts. Pam bid four hearts and that ended the auction of hand five.

Pam	Me
♠ 6	♠ J 10 9
♡ K Q J 9 8	♡ A 6
◇ A Q 10 9 8	◇ K J
♣ Q 3	♣ A K 9 7 5 2

We looked at each other's hands. She noticed at once we had a slam in three suits. "Dummy, why did you open one notrump with a six-card suit?" (In fairness, those "dummies" were said affectionately.)

My God, I thought, this is worse than the Reisinger. What have I gotten myself in for? Well, there were only three more hands. Maybe I'll survive. Sure.

Hand six looked simple enough. I picked up:

♠ K 10 5 2 ♡ K 7 ◇ A J 5 2 ♣ 10 9 3.

Pam opened one club and I responded one spade. She raised to two spades, which did not promise four-card support. I tried two notrump and Pam passed. Here are the two hands.

Pam	Me
♠ A 9 4 3	♠ K 10 5 2
♡ Q 8	♡ K 7
◇ Q 6 3	◇ A J 5 2
♣ K Q 6 2	♣ 10 9 3

Obviously we belonged in a spade part-score. "You have a doubleton heart," she said. "So do you," I countered. "I had honors in every suit (she pointed to them) and I thought it might play easier in notrump."

"Well, you could have been right, but not this time," I said as sweetly as possible. But it wasn't easy.

Only two more hands to go and I had my confidence back. I knew that Pam was upset that she hadn't taken me back to three spades and maybe, just maybe, we could bid these next two hands to the proper contract. Sure.

At this point Danny Rotman walked by and asked, "How many hands have you bid?" "Too many," said Pam. Her husband Jon was looking better and better to me all the time.

By now the other bridge players on the plane had heard some of these "dummies" coming from our section and were beginning to mosey over. A mutual friend of ours, Kay Schulle, leaned over her seat from two rows back to look at Pam's next hand—as if *Pam* were the one that needed moral support.

Hand seven. I picked up: ♠ Q ♡ 8 5 3 ◊ K J 10 9 5 ♣ A 7 6 3.

I passed and Pam opened one heart. We were playing "Drury." Playing Drury, if you are a passed hand and have support for partner's major plus a hand too strong to raise to two of partner's major, you respond two clubs, indicating a near opening hand, typically with three-card support.

I didn't think I was quite strong enough to Drury so I contented myself with a loud raise to two hearts. Pam bid four hearts which ended our thrilling auction.

Pam	Me
♠ A 8 5	♠ Q
♡ A K Q 7 4 2	♡ 8 5 3
◊ A Q	◊ K J 10 9 5
♣ 8 2	♣ A 7 6 3

Cold for seven. I braced myself. "Dummy, you have a Drury. We missed an 'easy' grand slam." This girl must have a twin sister who plays with Jon.

I didn't say anything but the thought crossed my mind that perhaps, just perhaps, she might have found some rebid other than four hearts with than junior two-bid. Reading my mind, I heard her say, "I had a balanced hand and couldn't visualize a slam when *all* you could bid was two hearts."

Before fateful hand eight, I decided to canvas some of the better players aboard to see whether or not they would Drury with my hand. Most said they would, including Kay Schulle, now entrenched in Pam's camp of supporters. However, Billy Eisenberg, bless him, said it was a "marginal Drury."

Well, we were finally ready for the very last hand. I wanted to end this bid-em-up on a happy note as I still had three hours left to spend with my understanding seat-mate.

Hand number eight. Neither side vulnerable and one spade is opened to my left. My hand: ♠ 5 3 ♡ Q 10 5 ◊ Q 5 3 2 ♣ J 7 6 2.

Pam overcalled two spades, describing a hand with five hearts and five or six cards in an unspecified minor.

I decided to make the non-forcing response of three hearts. This was greeted by three spades from Pam, a cue bid indicating slam interest.

I was definitely not interested in slam, so I signed off with four hearts. She now bid five clubs. The bidding had gone so far:

Me		Pam's sister	
West	North	East	South
—	1 ♠	2 ♠	pass
3 ♡	pass	3 ♠	pass
4 ♡	pass	5 ♣	pass
?			

What does the evil twin want from me now? This must be her second suit and she must have a whale of a hand. I didn't have many bids left in me, and I didn't want to hear any more affectionate "dummies," so I screwed up my courage and bid six clubs.

I figured it would play better in clubs than hearts because she would be able to discard a spade from my hand on one of her hearts after drawing trumps—assuming, of course, that she had the ace of spades.

I figured the bidding was over and was about to glance at her hand when I heard six diamonds from my left hand seat belt. (I had stopped looking at her after hand five.)

If I didn't know better I would have thought that Marshall Miles had snuck into her seat and made that bid. But Marshall didn't even go to the tournament. There was no doubt about it, I was sweating. What in the "&&## was she doing, and how could she possibly have stayed married to Jon for seventeen years, happily to boot?

Could diamonds be her second suit? If so, why didn't she bid diamonds first? I'm sure we belonged in her minor, but at the seven level?

I could no longer take any chances. I took my piece of paper and canvassed all the experts in First Class, Business, Economy, and Super Saver.

Most agreed with my actions so far and were pondering about what to do next. In the meantime, Pam was shaking her head mournfully. "How could they all be such dummies? Here I am bidding my hand so beautifully, and they don't know what I'm doing."

The longer it took everyone to bid, the better I felt. Well, here goes nothing. I bid seven clubs! If her suit was diamonds, let her correct. "Pass," she said. "Of course I have clubs, dummy." There it was. She had nailed me with the "d" word again. (Without even seeing my hand.)

"Could I just see your hand, Pam, dear?"

She looked up. "Pam, dear" had alerted her to possible trouble.

Pam's sister	Me
♠ A 7 6	♠ 5 3
♡ A K J 9 8	♡ Q 10 5
◊ —	◊ Q 5 3 2
♣ A K Q 9 8	♣ J 7 6 2

"Well," I said, "we can make it if clubs are 2-2." Kay Schulle piped up from Economy, "Clubs were 3-1." "We still make it if the hand with three clubs has four hearts." "The hand with three clubs did not have four hearts."

I fell back in my seat. Silence pervaded. Finally, Pam's sister said sweetly with a smile on her very pretty face, "Have any more bid-em-ups, Edwin?"

I should have taken the voucher.

At last, home again with Yvonne.

If you enjoyed this book, perhaps you'd like to read Eddie's regular column, Kantar's Korner, in the magazine, Bridge Today.

Bridge Today features many world-famous writers including some of the people in this book: Matthew Granovetter, Mike Lawrence, Al Roth and Alfred Sheinwold. It is a beautiful 6 by 9 inch format with large 10-point type as you see here. There are contests, puzzles, and huge discounts on other fine bridge books.

For a sample copy, send a check for $5 to:
Bridge Today, 18 Village View Bluff, Ballston Lake, NY 12019.
For a full one-year subscription (six issues), send $21.

Bridge Today makes a wonderful gift (even to yourself!)

Other recent selections from Granoveter Books include:

Murder at the Bridge Table by Matthew Granovetter
Called "Bridge Book of the Year" by Alfred Sheinwold, this improve your bridge/murder mystery combo is the first of its kind. $12.95

Tops and Bottoms by Pamela and Matthew Granovetter
A rare collection of 52 triumphs or disasters, reported by the world's leading players, includes postmortems by the authors. $11.95.

Spingold Challenge by Allan Falk
You find yourself in the finals of the Spingold Team Championship. The hands are difficult. Can you meet the challenge? $11.95.

Bridge Is A Partnership Game by Alvin Roth and Tobias Stone
The classic reprinted with a new chapter by Roth detailing the updates in The System. "The best book on bidding ever written." $13.95.